BOTTLED UP
SECRET

Visit us at www.boldstrokesbooks.com

BOTTLED UP SECRET

by

Brian McNamara

A Division of Bold Strokes Books

2014

CREDITS
EDITOR: JERRY WHEELER
PRODUCTION DESIGN: STACIA SEAMAN
COVER DESIGN BY GABRIELLE PENDERGRAST

This novel is dedicated to my closest high school friends, with whom I will always share my favorite memories.

Chapter One

Kelly Clarkson is blaring in my car as I make a left onto Farrow's Garden Path. This neighborhood is so big, it feels like a maze, but I've finally reached my destination. I pull into Kara's driveway and patiently wait. No need to honk—she always sees my headlights through her front windows. About thirty seconds later, she walks out of her house with that half-smile on her face.

"Hey!" I say as she opens the passenger door. "Do you hate that I'm always on time?"

"Sometimes, yes!" She pulls down the car visor to look at herself in the small mirror. "My hair's still a little wet, but whatever."

"Are you excited?!" I ask while reversing out of her driveway.

"I know *you* are. Do we know if it's going to be good?"

As one of my best friends, Kara knows that she is required to attend all of my high school musical theater performances. Tonight's show, however, will be different as I will be an audience member, not a performer. Leave it to my oldest sister to get married on the closing weekend of my senior year show. I'm still a little bitter I wasn't able to be part of it, but I'm pumped to see what my friends have in store tonight.

"I actually heard it's really good," I say. "And it's *42nd Street*—there's bound to be some good dancing."

"All right, all right. Wait, Brendan, when is your sister's wedding?"

"Next Saturday. Ugh."

I'm thankful for my big family, but sometimes having five older sisters can be a little overwhelming. In the past few years, I've realized how much closer I am to my friends than my family. Maybe that's normal for a seventeen-year-old. Regardless, hanging out with all of my relatives for hours on end at the wedding doesn't sound too appealing.

"That's right," Kara says. "But you're not a groomsman..."

"No, just walking her down the aisle. Oh! Are you still up for the cast party after the show?"

"Yeah, I'll do whatever. You drove, so I'll leave the night up to you."

"Sweet. Reese and Kelly said they'd go too, so you won't be alone." I'm hoping they stick to their word because I'll be preoccupied with my theater friends after the show. I don't want Kara to be a loner at the party.

A few minutes later, we pull into the St. Mary's High School for Girls parking lot for the show. I sometimes wonder what going to school with all of my girl friends would have been like. Would they have distracted me more than all the eye candy that I have at St. Xavier, my all-boys school?

"All right, let's do this," I say, suddenly getting nervous. For what, I'm not sure. "Reese texted me. She and Kelly are waiting in the lobby."

As I walk through the doors, I'm immediately impressed. The school has been working on the construction of a new theater for the past year or so, and it looks awesome. Tonight's show is the first performance in it, yet another reason to be bitter about not being onstage tonight.

"B!" I hear shouted across the room. Reese is walking toward me with Kelly trailing behind. Seeing them gets me even more excited.

"Hey! What's going on?" I say.

"In the past five minutes, we've seen about twelve people we know," Reese says.

"Eight of whom we'd be happy if we never saw again," Kelly

chimes in. I swear, Reese and Kelly are like a comedy duo. We've all been friends since first grade, but those two have done everything together: Girl Scouts, swim team, student council. I wouldn't say they look alike, but they do clock in at the same height, five-nine.

"Oh gosh," I say. "Earlier today I told Kara she better look good tonight because she's going to see everyone she knows." Before I can finish my thought, I see Mrs. Brewer, the mother of one of my classmates, walking toward me.

"Brendan! How are you?" She's actually a super-sweet woman and looks much younger than her age, due to her natural beauty. Her son and I were close friends when we were younger. You can tell a part of her wishes that he and I still hung out.

"Hi, Mrs. Brewer. I'm good. How are you?"

"I'm good. I always seem to find you in a swarm of women." She laughs. I hear that a lot and never really know what to say. Even my Theology teacher once said something similar to me in front of the whole class. He saw me at a football game and couldn't believe how many girls I was with.

Like many gay guys, I've always felt comfortable around girls. I chalk it up to growing up with a house full of women. That must be why I get along so well with them. Maybe that's partly true, but I could only tell myself that for so long before admitting the reason I only have platonic relationships with girls.

It's nice to have that burden lifted off my shoulders. Now if only I could get the courage to tell someone other than myself that I'm gay. It's not like I have any romantic prospects in my life, so I guess there's no rush in coming out.

"I thought you were in this show," Mrs. Brewer continues.

"No, my sister is getting married next weekend on closing night, so I wasn't able to do it."

"Which sister?" she asks, always wanting updates on my family. I'm waiting for the "How's your mom doing?" question. Even after six years, people are still concerned about her well-being following my dad's death. I can understand that; the pain never really goes away, even for me.

"Sarah," I tell her.

"Aw, good for her. That's so exciting. Well listen, tell your mom I say hello."

"Will do." I turn to my friends. "All right, are we ready?" The four of us find our seats and sift through our programs as we wait for the lights to go down.

"You guys still up for the cast party afterward?" I ask Reese and Kelly with considerably less confidence that they'll respond the way Kara did.

"Yeah, I think so," Reese says. "Will there be any cute, single guys there?"

"Correction," Kelly says. "Will there be any cute, single, *straight* guys there?"

"Straight slash questioning, yes."

"Good enough," Kelly says.

"It will be fun, I promise."

Throughout high school I've always been the planner in my group of friends. I've been known to push people together, remaining optimistic that the night will turn into fun for all. Fortunately, I'm usually right. We'll see how tonight goes.

Boom! As the bass drum hits and the trumpets flare, the lights quickly dim. It's showtime.

❖

As the cast is taking their bows a little over two hours later, the crowd is on their feet, and deservedly so. The dancing, the singing, and most of the acting were top notch.

"Go Natalie!" I yell to another member of our circle of friends as she comes onstage to take the final bow. As the curtain goes down and the crowd quiets, we scurry out to the lobby.

"That was so good," Kelly says as we wait for our friends to appear from backstage.

"I know. I loved it. See, these high school shows aren't so bad," I say, knowing that this production is definitely superior to the ones I've been in.

Chris is one of the first to appear from the double doors. He is a year younger than the rest of us, and is one of my only openly gay friends. It helps to have him as an example before I inevitably have to come out. The reaction from our friends regarding Chris has been really positive. This isn't surprising considering most of them are in theater. They're not the ones I'm worried about. My family is a different story. As Chris greets his parents, Natalie appears.

"Good job!" I exclaim as she runs toward me.

"Thanks. I expect a full rundown of your favorite parts of the show later."

"Obviously."

After hugging each of us, she moves on to her family while my friends and I make small talk with people we don't want to see and straight out avoid people we *really* don't want to see.

"All right, Reese. I need an update on this guy you're seeing," I say.

She's eager to share. "Okay, he plays guitar, which is really hot, he owns a Vespa, and he refuses to call me his girlfriend."

Kara and I laugh while Kelly chimes in with her practical yet harsh opinion. "Yeah, and he has no plans to attend college next year so…next!"

Unfazed, Reese continues. "Did I mention he has the most amazing jawline?"

"Is he Mr. Right?" I ask.

"He's Mr. Right Now," Reese says without missing a beat.

I laugh. "All right, I vote that it's time for us to head out. Thoughts?"

"Please," Kara says.

Nights like this remind me how much I'm going to miss everyone when we go off to college next year. We've known each other for over a decade and have definitely taken our proximity for granted. Next year, we'll no longer be able to drive five minutes to see each other. Our friendships will require real effort. Seeing who stays close to each other and whose friendships fade will be interesting.

Before leaving the theater, I motion to Natalie and Chris to let them know we are leaving. Chris gives me a nod to indicate that he will be heading out soon.

"So, what's Andrew up to tonight?" I ask Kara as she and I walk to my car.

"I think he's just hanging out at his friend's house."

It's not that I'm not a fan of her boyfriend. I just think she can do better. They've been dating for about a year now, but I've only hung out with him a handful of times.

Kara doesn't bring Andrew out with us much. Perhaps because she knows he's different than the rest of us. He's on the shy side and never really initiates conversation. When I do try to talk to him, he's very short with me. I guess I can understand if he doesn't feel like being thrown into a room of outgoing, loud, sarcastic people he barely knows, but he should make an effort to get to know his girlfriend's best friends.

I lead the way in my car while Reese and Kelly follow closely behind. The party is only a few minutes away, and based on the number of cars on the street, we are among the first to arrive. For my friends' sake, I tell them that we should wait in the car until more people get there. *I'll* know most people at the party, but they sure as heck won't.

About five minutes later, we walk into the house and are immediately ushered downstairs into the basement. Perhaps should have given it *ten* minutes. With a pool table to the left and a couch and TV in the distance, the partygoers still have plenty of floor space. I turn to my right and see a spread of pizza, snacks, and pop, which I will definitely be hitting up shortly.

I immediately feel at home, mingling with my fellow thespians. The three musketeers, on the other hand, awkwardly move to the corner until they can get a good feel for the scene. I'm still impressed they all actually came to the party.

"Brendan!" I hear from across the room. I see Cory, a girl who may or may not have had a crush on me junior year. A girl whom I may or may not have inadvertently led on. While I thought we were forming a strong friendship, she saw the situation a little differently. I sometimes forget no one knows I'm gay.

"How's it going?" I ask. "Great job tonight."

"Thanks. I wish you could have been in it."

"I know. It's such a fun show. I enjoyed being in the audience, though."

"Hey, do you know if you're doing any of the acting classes at the Buckley Center next year?"

"Good question. They start in January?"

She nods.

"The Acting for TV class sounds fun but I'm sure it's hard to get into," I say.

"I'm going to do the improv class. You should do it too."

Before we can finish our conversation, Natalie and Chris come down the basement staircase with Mark Galovic, a fellow classmate who, like Chris, is only a junior. Although I've never officially met him before, I've admired him in the halls plenty of times.

The kid is beautiful. His dirty blond hair, blue eyes, and somewhat larger nose give him that European look. He's an avid soccer player, so I can only imagine how good he looks with his clothes off. Other than being friends with Chris, I'm not really sure why he would be at this party. Plus, he and Chris aren't super close—more just friends at school as opposed to weekend buddies. As the two of them head to get some food, Natalie and I meet in the center of the room.

I've known Natalie since first grade too, and she's probably my only friend who truly understands my sense of humor. If I tell an outrageous joke, she'll call me weird but will then immediately take the joke to a new level.

She likes to think she's Carrie Bradshaw from *Sex and the City*. I have to admit they do have some similarities: short, same petite yet curvy body type, and even the signature long curly hair, although Natalie's is jet black. Like Carrie, Natalie can also always come up with something witty on the spot.

"Brendan," she says with a serious face—well, as serious as Natalie gets.

"Yes."

"We need to talk."

"What's up?"

"Do you know Mark?" She slyly looks over her right shoulder to ensure he is not within earshot.

"Technically, yes," I say, curious to find out where she's going with this.

"Okay, his younger sister is in the show, so he came to see it last night."

"Okay…"

"So Chris convinced him to come to the cast party afterward, and he and I flirted the whole time. We were dancing together, he told me I was beautiful, and then we exchanged numbers."

"Why am I hearing about this just now?"

"So we texted today, and I told him that he should come to the party tonight, and here he is!"

I've got to give it to Natalie. She is so funny and outgoing and makes amazing first impressions. Guys always respond to it. I do get sad from time to time because I don't have experiences like this. The closest I've come to dating someone is when I had a crush on my friend last year. He's even gay, too, but in the end I was too scared to tell him, so nothing happened. Still, it was nice to feel butterflies.

As Natalie goes on about her night with Mark, I try to act interested, but not too interested. Remember, I'm still putting up a front. As much as I agree with her when she talks about how hot he is, I give a slight smile.

"That's so exciting," I say, suddenly noticing Kara, Reese, and Kelly playing pool with a couple of others. I'm glad to see that they're having fun. Reese motions for us to come over.

"We'll see what happens tonight," Natalie says as we head over to them.

"You want the next game with Kara?" Reese asks me.

"Sure."

"Okay, you guys will play the winners of this round."

I notice that she and Kelly are playing against two guys who were part of the orchestra tonight. My friends look like they're going to lose, but their opponent scratches on the eight ball, and they miraculously pull through. Now it's my turn to dethrone them.

Kara and I start clearing the table like it's our job. With two striped balls remaining for us to sink, compared to our opponents' six solid-colored balls, I notice Chris and Mark join the group of spectators. Kelly is up and attempts to hit the yellow one ball into a corner pocket but misses. I chalk up my stick and go for the twelve ball. Sunk. Next up is the fourteen. Done. All that's left is the eight ball.

"Be careful, Brendan," Reese says. "This is where we usually win. Don't let the pressure get to you."

I bend down and angle my stick to trace a path. "Side pocket," I say before striking. Well, I sank the ball…the *cue* ball. Scratch.

"Yes!" Reese and Kelly high-five each other.

I reach out my arm to shake their hands. "Great job, you guys. You really earned it," I say in a sarcastic tone.

"I know how much you two hate losing," Reese says with a smile.

"We're not used to it," Kara responds. "You guys, on the other hand…"

It's true. Kara and I are pretty competitive. I swear we're not sore losers, but our blood pressure rises a little bit when we compete.

"Who's next?" Kelly says. As they choose their next victims, Kara and I get some food.

About thirty minutes later, the music is pumping and the party is still hopping. A small dance floor has even formed in front of the TV. While I'm snacking with Kara, I notice one of my theater friends dancing. She and I actually share the same last name, but we're not related. As our eyes meet, she waves me over to join the dance crew.

"Get over here, Brendan Madden. If *he* knows this song, I know *you* do." Suddenly I notice the "he" she's referring to—Mark. As he turns to smile at me, I start to walk over, suddenly getting nervous. I attempt to seamlessly dance myself into the group but feel self-conscious.

"You guys know each other, right?" my friend asks us.

"Um…" I say.

"Kind of," Mark says.

"Yeah, how's it going?" I finish.

His beauty is breathtaking up close. His eyes couldn't be any bluer, his skin couldn't be any clearer, and I hadn't noticed his nice, full lips before.

As the mob of dancers moves around, I suddenly find myself cornered off with him. It seems awkward to keep dancing, so he and I decide to gradually stop and talk instead.

"So, I heard you went to the cast party yesterday," I say.

"Yeah, it was…interesting," he says, flashing his gorgeous smile.

I laugh. "These parties always are."

"Wait, you weren't in the show tonight, were you?"

"No, my sister's getting married next weekend, unfortunately, so I couldn't do it."

"Unfortunately." He laughs.

"Unfortunately for *me*," I clarify. "I even asked her if I could show up late to the reception so I could still do the show. She considered it for a second but then was like, 'Wait, what? No!'" He laughs again. "And your sister's in the show, right? Is she here?"

"Yeah, she's over there in the yellow shirt," he says, pointing across the room. Once I spot her, I can't believe I didn't notice the resemblance earlier in the night. They both have the same blond hair and tall, athletic build.

As I search for the next topic of conversation, I realize how pleasantly surprised I am by Mark's demeanor. I would expect someone so good-looking to have a pompous attitude. So far, he'd been nothing but kind and sincere.

"So, do you live on the west side?" I ask. Almost everyone I know lives in the suburbs of Cleveland as opposed to downtown. I'm about a fifteen-minute drive west of the city. My high school is in Cleveland proper, so Mark could just as easily live on the east side, but I'm hoping he lives in my part of town.

"Yeah, I'm in Rocky River," he responds.

"Oh, nice. Not far from me at all."

"Yeah, you live near Chris, right?"

"Yep, just a few streets away. I'm his chauffeur to school every day."

"Oh, that explains why he's always late," he says, smiling.

"What? No way. I pull into his driveway at seven-fifteen every day. *He's* the one who makes *me* wait."

"Kidding, kidding."

"Wait, do you even have first period with Chris?"

He nods. "French with Mr. Trumble."

"I have him too."

"He's crazy, right?" Mark says. "In a good way."

"Crazy slash terrifying."

"Slash hard. The oral exams are so tough."

"See, I'm actually good at the oral stuff." His eyes widen as I realize what I just said.

"Whoa, T.M.I., Brendan," he says. "We barely know each other."

I bow my head down and cover it with my hand as I feel my cheeks getting red. He grabs my shoulders and shakes me a little bit. "I'm just messing with you." Feeling him touch me ensures that the color in my cheeks will remain for a few more seconds. I look back up at him anyway.

"So, what grade do you usually get on these oral exams?" he asks with a straight face.

"You know, it depends how much I practice," I say, matching his seriousness.

"Okay, well maybe you can give me some pointers."

"Absolutely. It's actually all about the tongue pla—okay, I'm done," I say, finally cracking.

"I win. And I know how much you hate to lose," he says, referring to my bad luck at the billiards table earlier.

"I choked. Too many eyes were on me."

"How are you so good at pool?"

"I have a table at home, but I really don't play much."

"Well, I was impressed. I'm thirsty. Want to get something to drink?"

"Yeah, let's go."

I don't have any close straight male friends, so I don't know if the conversation I just had with Mark is considered normal. I know we were talking and joking around, but the gleam in his eye made it seem like flirting. Or maybe I'm just delusional. Either way, I'm feeling major butterflies right now.

As soon as Mark and I start walking toward the counter, Natalie and Chris spot us. The dance floor offered us some sort of secret, secluded space that we may not get back the rest of the night.

"Brendan," Chris says.

"I feel like I haven't talked to you all night, Chris. How's it going?"

"Okay, Brendan," Natalie interrupts. "Time for you to tell us your favorite parts of the show."

"They did this to me in the car," Mark whispers to me. "Just say 'the dancing.'"

"You can get away with that," I say. "They expect a detailed review from me."

"Yes, we do," Natalie says.

"Okay, first off, I loved the show as a whole—the style of music, the corny storyline, the *dancing*." I give a smile to Mark. "The number toward the end was amazing. And I liked your song with Dorothy," I say to Natalie. "That was cute."

My answer seems to have satisfied them, but I'm sure we'll revisit the topic later. I do this with my friends after they see shows that I'm in. I'm always curious what sticks out as highlights.

"How do you know these two?" Mark asks me.

"Grade school. Natalie I've known since first grade. Chris… well, I don't know. When did we first meet?"

"Good question. I was friends with Natalie before you. Probably like sixth grade. You were in seventh. But I feel like we didn't really start to be friends until I shadowed you at Xavier."

"Oh yeah. I remember not even volunteering for that. One morning someone knocked on the door of my first-period class and was like, 'Brendan Madden, we have an eighth grader here who's going to follow you around today.'"

"Yep, that was my mom's doing," Chris says. "It's because

Mrs. Hansen said you remind her of me so my mom felt like I'd be in good hands."

"And you were," I say with a smile to feign modesty.

"Who's Mrs. Hansen?" Mark asks.

"Our eighth-grade teacher," I respond. "Sorry, are we going too fast for you?"

"Yes, I'm the outsider."

"I'm right there with you tonight," I say. "I don't know half the people here."

I look at my watch and notice that it's already twenty after twelve. I don't have a curfew, but I never really stay out too late. Maybe because my weekends usually consist of low-key events, such as going to Applebee's for their late-night, half-priced appetizers or seeing a movie at a local theater. Pretty badass stuff.

After about ten more minutes of conversation, I make eye contact with Kara and see if she's ready to go. She nods. After I go around the room saying my good-byes, I end back at Chris, Natalie, and Mark.

"See you, Brendan," Chris says before we embrace.

As Natalie gives me a hug, she whispers into my ear, "I'll call you tomorrow with an update." Sure, some part of me will be jealous to hear the details of her interactions with Mark, but it's also fun to live vicariously through her. And I'd rather have all information relating to him as opposed to being in the dark.

I then turn to Mark. "Good seeing you," I say.

"You too. See you soon I'm sure."

Maybe it was because I was on a hugging spree or maybe my body overtook my brain, but seemingly without control, I lift my arms up and go in for a hug. Thankfully, he does the same. As I pull his body into mine, I feel a jolt of electricity. I don't know how he's done it, but I've fallen hard for this guy after one night.

CHAPTER TWO

B rendan?" I open my eyes the next morning and see my mom peering through the crack of my bedroom door. "Natalie's on the phone."

"What time is it?" I ask in a barely audible voice.

"Ten-thirty." Not too early, but I could have used another thirty minutes. I keep my cell on silent at night so I can avoid unwanted wake-up calls.

My mom hands me our house phone. "Why are you up so early?" I immediately ask Natalie. She usually doesn't get up before noon on the weekends.

"I have no idea. Probably because I've been waiting to spill all the details from last night to you and whoever else will listen."

"But I was there. What could have possibly happened?"

Natalie proceeds to tell me how Mark went out of his way to drive her home last night. In the car, they apparently chatted and flirted nonstop. She tells me the details of their conversation and how charming he was. I'm happy to hear that the car ride concluded with a hug and not a kiss.

"So then I texted him after he dropped me off, thanking him for the ride," she says. "He texted back, saying 'Anytime' with a smiley face."

Big deal. *She's* the one who texted first. Gosh, what's my problem? I feel so catty. I'm usually very supportive of my friends, but my competitive spirit is coming out the more Natalie talks about

Mark. I feel such a strong sense of jealousy, although I make sure she doesn't notice.

"That's awesome," I tell her.

"Oh, I'm also calling because a group of us is going to that coffee shop, Cravings, today if you want to go. I know, I know, you don't drink coffee."

I don't ask who's going, although all I can wonder is if Mark will be there.

"What time?" I ask.

"Two."

"Okay, so you'll get there at what, two-twenty?" She's notorious for being late.

"Sounds about right."

"All right, I'll be there."

After getting dressed and brushing my teeth, I head downstairs where I'm greeted by my two dogs, a black lab and a teacup poodle. It's an odd pairing but it works. The poodle is actually the more aggressive of the two, trying to overcompensate.

"What time did you get home last night?" my mom asks.

And it begins. She never used to ask many questions about my social life, but lately it's been like an inquisition: Where did you go? Who was there? Who are you texting?

My mom and I have never been that close. Ever since my dad died, she sort of checked out as a parent. Before I knew it, all of my sisters were out of the house, so it was just the two of us. As I got older, my mom would comment on any signs of femininity or so-called "gayness" that I displayed. Every time she did that, I suppressed my true self more and more.

Without realizing it, I slowly adopted two personas: a fun, outgoing, happy-go-lucky person who doesn't take life too seriously when he's with his friends, and a quiet, boring person when he's with his family. It wasn't a conscious decision, but I don't want to give my mom anything to evaluate or criticize me about.

It's been working just fine until recently. She seems to be suspicious about everything I do. She knows that I don't drink or do drugs, so it has nothing to do with that. I'm scared that her fear of my being gay has turned into her *belief* that I'm gay, and she's trying to dig deeper each time she interrogates me. I haven't even thought of how I'd have the coming-out conversation with her, mostly because I don't plan on having it any time soon.

"I got back at, like, twelve forty-five," I answer.

"Where did you go after the play?"

"The cast party."

"Whose house was it at?"

"Just this girl from the show. I don't know her."

As I start to pour some cereal into a bowl, I'm waiting for normal questions like, "How was the show? Did you have fun? Were your friends good in it?" But the questioning is over.

After some TV and lounging around, I get ready for the afternoon get-together. I'm usually a low-maintenance guy, but today I'm paying extra attention to how I look due to a certain someone I might see. I've picked out some jeans, but I only own two pairs so it wasn't hard. I'm not having much success with a shirt, though. I finally settle on a long-sleeve red and white baseball tee.

Now on to my hair. It's the usual disheveled mess, but today I'm whipping out the hair product. With a little twist, a few pulls, and a couple flicks, it doesn't look half bad. I decide to stop before really messing it up.

I pull into the Cravings parking lot at about two-ten, halfway between the meeting time and Natalie's expected arrival. Although it's a popular local coffee shop, I've actually never been inside before. I open the pink door, walk in, and look around for a familiar face. I still don't know who will be here, but I assume Chris and other theater people. I suddenly spot him, Kelly, and a few others.

As I smile and head over, I notice Mark sitting across from Chris, looking even better than last night if that's possible. Next to him is an empty seat. Would sitting there be too obvious, or should I take one of the other available chairs? I decide to be bold.

"It's our fan club!" Chris says as I sit down.

"You know it!"

"Perfect timing," Chris continues. "We're playing a game where someone throws out a question and we all have to answer it."

"Also known as a conversation," I say jokingly. "Okay, what's the question now?"

"If you had to hook up with a celebrity of the same sex, who would it be?"

"I wonder who thought of that one."

"Guilty," Chris says.

"Wait a minute, that's too easy for you," I say to him.

"No, no, I had to pick a girl. All right, Kelly, your turn."

"Okay. Alicia Silverstone."

"What?" Chris and I say in unison.

"What?" she says, slightly embarrassed.

"That's so random," I say. "Is she still even considered a celebrity?"

"Yeah," Chris says, "have you thought about this before today?"

"What the hell?" Kelly says. "I was trying to think outside the box and I love *Clueless*. All right, next."

"You know we won't let you live that down," Chris says to her. "All right, Mark, you're up."

Like Chris, I'm on pins and needles waiting to hear what he'll say. The two of them are just friends, but I remember Chris talking about how he wishes Mark were gay or even that he suspects that Mark is gay. I never paid much attention because I hadn't met Mark before. Of course now I'm kicking myself for not remembering every detail of what Chris said. I want to know if I have a shot with this kid.

"I don't know who to pick," Mark says with a smile on his face, clearly not wanting to answer.

"Mark..." Chris warns.

"Okay, um...Taylor Lautner?"

"Hot," Chris says. "All right, Brendan..." I can tell that Chris is anxiously awaiting my answer as well. I have no doubt he thinks I'm gay. We've known each other long enough for him to suspect.

I take a few seconds to think of a hot blond celebrity who

resembles Mark to subtly let him know what my type is. Plus, I don't want to answer too quickly. Suddenly it hits me.

"David Beckham," I say, perhaps too excitedly. Not only is he a hot blond, he's a hot blond soccer player, just like Mark.

"Interesting," Chris says.

The game continues with an array of questions, including the age at which you had your first kiss, your most embarrassing moment, and the last one—what's your dream college? This question segues into a side conversation between Mark and me.

"So, do you know where you're going to school next year yet?" he asks.

"No idea. Well, I have an idea. I got into Georgetown and Ohio State, which are two of the frontrunners, but I'm waiting to hear from a couple others. I do know that I want a big school in more of a city as opposed to a college town. I know you're only a junior, but do you plan on playing soccer in college or what?"

"Yeah, I hope so. I'll probably have to go to a smaller school, though…in a college town."

I laugh. "Okay, so we know we won't be going to the same school."

"You're not planning on playing tennis next year?"

"No, no, no. I got burnt out when I was fourteen," I say, wondering how he even knows that I play. I guess I've gotten a good amount of publicity for it at school and in the paper. I started playing when I was really young and have had a successful competitive tennis career, but I can't picture myself continuing after this year. "Maybe intramural tennis," I add.

"We should play sometime," he says. Did he really just ask me to hang out?

"Oh, do you play?"

"Not really." He flashes me that adorable smile of his. "Well, I've played before, but I've never taken lessons or anything."

"I could teach you. Just not sure if you can afford my hourly rate."

"You're that good, huh?"

"Yeah, but I'll go easy on you."

I know my gaydar is usually a little overeager, but again I'm getting the feeling that Mark is flirting with me. Each time he smiles, his eyes turn into these beautiful pools of blue. They are hypnotizing.

Chris overhears our conversation and decides to give Mark a warning. "Mark, don't play tennis with Brendan. He's too good; it's ridiculous."

"No," I say unconvincingly. "I can bring my game down for others." *Don't screw this up for me, Chris*, I think.

"Mark, you know he got third in state last year, right?"

"Seriously?" Mark asks me, his face stunned. "I didn't know you were *that* good."

"I got lucky."

"Oh, right," Mark says. "Third place in Division One tennis. Luck. And you're really not playing in college?"

I shake my head. "It's too much of a commitment. I like it, but not enough. I want time to do other things, like theater."

"Okay, so you're a tennis pro and will probably *win* states this year, you're great at singing and acting, you're an expert billiards player…what else can you impress me with?"

"Hmm."

Chris butts in again. "Brendan has never had a drop of alcohol in his life and says he never will."

"What the heck," I say. "Where did that come from?"

"I'm just sharing interesting facts about you," Chris says in an innocent tone, although I know he's trying to embarrass me.

"I don't drink either," Mark says, smiling at me.

"Nice."

"Why never, though?" he asks.

"Okay, this is going to sound ridiculous, but do you remember the DARE program?"

"Like in fifth grade? Yeah."

"Well, they said that we shouldn't smoke or do drugs, and I thought, 'Okay, that's a no-brainer.' Then they also said that we shouldn't drink alcohol because it kills brain cells. So being the logical fifth grader I was, I thought, 'Well, that's not good. I'm never going to drink, then.'"

Mark laughs. "Simple as that, huh?"

"Yes. I understand now the reason is stupid, but I made a promise to myself back then that I would never do it. I don't have a problem with drinking, though." Chris clears his throat to disagree. "Okay, fine. I might be a little judgmental. I'm getting better, though. I just don't think it's necessary, especially for high schoolers."

"Wow," Mark says. "You're every parent's dream."

"Give him a few years," Chris says.

"Not convinced?" Mark replies.

"Brendan says he won't do a lot of things."

"Chris..." I warn. I know where he's going with this.

"What else?" Mark asks, intrigued.

Chris looks at me, debating whether to continue. "Oh, you don't care," he says to me.

"I'm not ashamed of it, but he barely knows me!"

"I won't judge, I promise," Mark says.

"Brendan's a virgin and is waiting until marriage," Chris blurts out. "Well, he *says* he's waiting until marriage."

"Okay, first off," I say, "Chris is a virgin too, so it's not like that's a big deal."

"Oh, agreed," Mark says. "I'm a virgin."

"Really?" Chris says. "You and Amy never had sex?" Mark shakes his head. Amy? Who is Amy? Don't even tell me he has a girlfriend. I almost ask about her but decide against it.

"And second," I continue, "I'm waiting to have *sex* until marriage, but as for everything else, I'm all for it if it's in the context of a relationship."

"Okay, that makes sense," Mark says. "I don't think that's *that* extreme."

"Thank you."

"Give him a few years," Chris says.

"Do you realize that the more you doubt me, the more I feel the need to prove you wrong? Although I must admit I'm more likely to budge on the 'no sex' thing than the 'no drinking' thing."

"Let's hope so," Chris says.

"Okay, enough about me, please. Chris, reveal something about Mark."

"Chris has got nothing on me," Mark says, unfazed.

"Seriously," Chris replies. "Mark is so secretive. I don't know about any of his skeletons."

"Okay, fine. Mark, reveal something about yourself. Anything."

He purses his big lips and looks up.

I can tell he's not going to come up with anything good so I say, "Actually, tell me about Amy. Your girlfriend?"

"*Ex*-girlfriend." Thank God. "We dated for about a year."

"When did you break up?"

"A few months ago. Right before school started."

I don't know whether to prod further. "Can I ask why?"

"It just wasn't right. I don't know. Something felt off."

Our conversation is interrupted when Natalie makes her fashionably late entrance. After saying hi to everyone, she pulls up a chair near me. Well, looks like I won't have any more alone time with Mark today. That's okay. Although I'm having a great time with him, this news about Amy lessens my hopes that he is gay anyway.

I start to think about where I was a year ago when *I* was a junior. I hadn't even admitted to myself that I was gay yet. If Mark really is gay, he hasn't come to terms with it. And if and when he does, he definitely won't be ready to tell anyone. All of my close friends are girls or gay guys, and *I'm* not even ready to tell anyone. With that said, I'm not sure I'm ready to give up on my crush just yet.

After talking and laughing with my friends for another hour, I head home to get cracking on a stack of homework I have waiting for me. This weekend was a blast, but tomorrow I go back to reality.

❖

The following Saturday is my sister's wedding. Fortunately, the ceremony goes off without a hitch. I escort her down the aisle without either one of us tripping, which is all I could ask for. I'm able to be more open with some of my sisters compared to my mom, but not by much. It helps that they are closer to my age, but that also means they are more likely to pick up on gay clues. I feel myself unconsciously playing it straight, not that my normal self is really flamboyant.

At the reception, I'm seated at a table with my twenty-two-year-old sister, Colleen, and her boyfriend, Kyle. I don't usually like guys that my sisters date, but Kyle is actually really cool. He is super outgoing and funny.

"All right, Brendan, give me the lowdown on colleges," he says. It's the question of the night. I guess it's the most obvious topic of conversation for a senior in high school.

"I have all my applications in, but I want to wait until the chips fall before I stress out about it too much." My stock response.

"I'm thinking Georgetown is the one," he says. "You'd fit perfectly in DC. You know I went to school in Baltimore."

"Oh yeah?"

My sister chimes in to brag about me. "Kyle, did I tell you about Brendan's Ohio State scholarship?" He shakes his head. "He had to do this essay competition in Columbus and got a full ride from it."

"Nice, Brendan!" he says.

"Thanks, but it's not a full ride. It was just a full academic scholarship. I still have to pay room and board. Some people got actual full rides."

"*And* he got into the honors program there," Colleen says to Kyle.

"That's not that hard to get into," I add.

"Brendan, stop," she says. "I'm so excited for you. You're going to have so much fun wherever you go. And I know the girls are going to go crazy over you."

Oh boy. Of all my sisters, I would expect Colleen to wonder

just a little about my sexuality, but I really don't think she does. Maybe because she's never had any gay friends, so she has no one to whom she can compare me. I figured having almost exclusively female or gay friends and being an active musical theater performer would be enough for anyone to at least suspect.

Any time talk of girls or dating comes up, I use my usual tactic and change the subject. "When is the reception over?" I ask Colleen. "Do you know?"

"I think eleven."

My question has ulterior motives behind it. Tonight is closing night of *42nd Street*, and I have an unconfirmed report that Mark will be attending the cast party afterward. The party won't be starting until about ten-thirty, so this might work out perfectly.

"All right, everyone, can I have your attention?" I hear from the DJ. "We're going to do some speeches to get this night of celebration kicked off, starting with Sarah's beautiful maid of honor, Jessica. Give her a round of applause, everyone."

We clap as she stands up, visibly nervous. Jessica has been friends with my sister for as long as I can remember. She's always been so nice and fun to have around.

"Hi, everyone," she says. "I want to start off by saying how happy I am for Sarah and Rob. I've always been very protective of my best friend, and I wasn't going to allow someone less than amazing to be with her. Fortunately, Rob, you bring out a light in Sarah's eyes like I've never seen. You are kind, loving, and supportive, which is all I've ever wanted for her.

"As some of you know, Sarah and I have known each other a very long time. I spent so much time at her house growing up that at times I felt like I was part of the Madden family, which was an honor for me.

"The other day," Jessica continues, "I was looking through some old things that I saved from when I was younger, and I stumbled across a letter that Sarah gave me. It was written when we were in seventh grade, so it talked about the usual vital things to a thirteen-year-old girl's life—boys, clothes, our upcoming science test. I couldn't contain my laughter as I pictured us writing these notes back and forth, not knowing what the future held for each of us. At the end of the letter, Sarah wrote three letters before signing her name—BFF…best friends forever.

"As I stand here today, almost twenty years later, I realize that as young and naïve as we were, we knew our friendship would never change. Sarah, as our lives get increasingly complicated and busy, and as we embark on new journeys of marriage and motherhood, I want you to know that I will always be here for you as your best friend, forever."

I notice tears coming to my sister's eyes as Jessica concludes her speech. It takes a lot for me to cry but even *I'm* trying to hold back tears. I can't help but compare the friendship that my sister has with Jessica to the bonds that I have with my friends. They've been right by my side during my childhood and now adolescence. I can only hope that they'll be there throughout my adulthood as well.

The reception continues for the next few hours with plenty of food and dancing. Before I know it, Donna Summer's "Last Dance" starts to play, signaling the end of the evening. I'm exhausted but still set on going to the cast party. After a few good-byes and a quick explanation to my mom, I leave the reception, arriving at the party at about eleven-twenty.

As I park my car and step out, my insanity hits me. I left my sister's wedding to race over to this party solely for the purpose of seeing a guy that I've technically known for one week. Obsessed much? I walk in and head to the living room where I see Natalie and…Yes. He's here. Sitting next to her, of course.

"Oh my gosh," Natalie says after spotting me. "Are you kidding me? You're still wearing your tux?"

"I know. I forgot to bring a change of clothes."

"How was the wedding?!"

"It was good, actually. I had fun." I make eye contact with Mark. "Hey, Mark, what's up?"

He flashes his smile with a "Hey."

"How was the show?" I ask Natalie.

"Um, kind of a mess."

"Oh no."

"No, it was fine. The audience didn't notice, but we were definitely distracted. Here, sit down. I was just about to go to the bathroom." I take her spot on the cramped couch and find myself sitting dangerously close to the blond hottie. There's even leg-to-leg contact. This couldn't have worked out better.

"Man, you're like a groupie," I say to Mark, trying to get in as much conversation with him as possible before Natalie returns.

"Look who's talking," he says, nudging my leg with his.

"Touché. What's going on? Having fun?"

"Yep, can't complain. Got here a little bit ago. You excited for our two-day week?"

"I am." I've been so preoccupied with family and wedding stuff, I almost forgot that Thanksgiving is coming up. "What do you do for the holiday?"

"We go to my grandparents'."

"Where do they live?"

"East side. Know where University Heights is?"

"Um…all right, I'm not even going to pretend to know. If it's not the west side, I have no idea."

He laughs. "You're funny. Are you going to the movie with everyone next weekend? It's on the west side."

"Plans next weekend already? I'm so out of the loop. What movie?"

"Natalie said she and some others are seeing…crap, I forget what it's called. The one with Jude Law."

I don't remember the name of the movie either, but that's because I have absolutely no desire to see it. Of course I respond, "Nice, I'm in."

Before I know it, Natalie returns. "Can I squeeze in here?" she asks. Mark scoots closer to me to make room for her. My leg-to-leg has turned into full side body contact with him.

"Keep scooting," Natalie says, needing a little more room. Mark moves his arm from his side to the cushion behind me, inching even closer. The feel of his bicep pushing against the back of my head is amazing.

"Theater people don't have regard for personal space, Mark," Natalie says. "Get used to it."

"I'm comfortable," he says.

"Brendan, guess what I just thought of," Natalie says.

"What?"

"The lockdown at St. Luke's."

"Oh my gosh. One of the worst nights of my high school life."

"What exactly does a lockdown entail?" Mark asks.

Natalie starts the recap. "Our grade school was having this Saturday night sleepover at the school, and they locked the doors so no one could leave. They had karaoke and a bunch of games for us to play. It was part of their Catholic youth group."

"It was all Kelly's fault, by the way," I say. "She was the only one involved in that group and she encouraged us to go."

"How bored were we that night to agree to that?"

"I don't know. The best part is we had to have our parents sign a permission slip, but, of course, my mom was out of town or something, so I had to forge it."

"That's right. But your handwriting is terrible, so it was painfully obvious it was fake."

"Did they figure it out?" Mark asks.

"Well, after practicing on scratch paper, I realized that it was hopeless," I say.

"So he made *me* forge the signature," Natalie says. Mark laughs. "Instead of it looking like a sixteen-year-old boy's signature, it looked like a sixteen-year-old *girl's* signature."

"We go to turn in our forms," I continue, "and the woman says to me, 'I want you to sign your mom's signature on this piece of paper because I think that *you* signed this form.' I signed it and showed her, and she was like, 'Oh, okay. I stand corrected.'"

"Meanwhile, I'm there thinking, 'Crap. She's going to ask *me* to sign it now,'" Natalie says.

"Did she?" Mark asks.

"No. I wish she had because what Brendan and I experienced next was terrible. We got about one hour of sleep on a cement floor and were freezing the whole night."

"Then the next day, we were all supposed to go to mass together," I say. "We dodged out of there instead, right?"

"Yes. I would have fallen asleep in the pew."

I spend the next hour or so trying to figure out whether Mark is flirting with me. All signs point to yes, but I wonder what an observer would think. Regardless, I have a great time talking and laughing with him. The more we interact, the faster the butterflies in my stomach flutter.

❖

A few days later, Thanksgiving break officially begins. I'm looking forward to the next time I can see Mark and the rest of my friends, but first I have to get through some family time. At home I slip into my boring, reserved personality, which allows me to avoid most personal questions asked by my sisters. When I really think about it, it's sad that I can't be myself in front of my family. I guess it's partly my fault because I control how I act around them and how much I let them in.

In my defense, when I display glimpses of my true self to them, I often get shot down or criticized. For example, if my mom sees me watching a show that a typical guy may not watch, such as *Will & Grace*, she tells me to change the channel and makes me feel ashamed for wanting to watch it. Most kids my age try to hide things like alcohol consumption from their parents; I hide my TV viewing habits.

When it comes to my friends, my sister once said to me, "I think you need to find more friends that are guys. You don't have that much in common with these girls that you hang out with, and it's important to have men as friends." It was clear she was afraid I might be gay. That always seems to be the reason for any comments from them.

"I never knew anyone like you when I was in high school," another one of my sisters said to me. I took this as a compliment but wasn't sure what she meant by it. Either way, it was another sign that I was coming off as different from a "normal" high school guy. The safest thing to do was to adjust my behavior to match their expectations of me.

On Thanksgiving day, my family and I put a time capsule together. I got some kit a year ago but never got around to coordinating it. Now that everyone is home for the holiday, I figure it's a perfect time. The instructions say to put in pictures, movie stubs, receipts or whatever, but the most fun part is to write down where you think you will be when the time capsule is opened.

My oldest sister, Sarah, was pushing hard to open it five years from now. She claimed she couldn't picture herself past the age of forty, so it must be opened before she gets over the hill. After some arguing, we decide that ten years is long enough for significant changes to happen in all of our lives. That will put Sarah at age forty-one. I'm surprised she still agreed to write something.

I sit with a pen and paper in my hands, not quite knowing where to start. In ten years, I'll be twenty-seven years old. I can imagine what it will be like when high school is over, but post-college? God knows what I'll be doing. I'm still trying to decide on a college major, let alone a career.

How about my love life? In ten years, I'm sure I'll be out to all of my friends and even my family. The thought stresses me out. How would I tell my family? Sit them all in a room? Call each of my sisters up on the phone? Can't I just do it through email?

Regardless, I hope to be in a relationship. I don't think I'll be married yet, and I definitely won't have kids. Maybe if we did a fifteen-year time capsule…Where will I live? I like Ohio, but I'm hoping to eventually leave. Maybe Chicago?

With no ink on the paper, I realize that my future is completely uncertain. Career, love life, location—who knows? It's exciting because I have my whole future ahead of me, but it's also scary. I don't want to wake up in ten years and realize I'm not where I want to be.

Perhaps to avoid disappointment, I keep my writing brief and vague: I want to be in a relationship, living in a major city, working at a job that I like. I also throw in a few of my favorite high school memories.

CHAPTER THREE

The day after a lazy Thanksgiving, movie night arrives and I'm beyond excited. The movie's going to be terrible, but who cares? I'll be seeing Mark tonight.

My friends always make fun of my taste in movies and music. "Brendan likes bad things," they tell others. Or "The movie was so good...you'd hate it, Brendan."

According to me, a movie needs to meet a few criteria in order for it to be good. First, it needs to be less than two hours, lest my undiagnosed ADD kick in. Second, it needs to not be boring. I'd much prefer seeing a comedy or suspense film, which usually holds my interest, as opposed to something like a historical drama. Finally, it needs to have good actors in it. It wouldn't hurt if these actors are hot as well.

I pull into the theater two minutes before my friends and I agreed to meet and find that I'm the first one to arrive. As I'm waiting outside, I see Kelly walk up.

"Where's Reese?" I ask her.

"I don't know."

"Oh, you didn't come together?"

"No, Brendan. She and I don't do everything together," she says, trying to sound annoyed, but her slight smile gives her away. "All right, that's a lie. Yeah, we do. She's here. She just ran into CVS."

I laugh. "Of course."

A few minutes later, as Reese walks our way, I get a text from an unknown number. It reads, "Hey, are you there yet?"

"Who is this?" I ask Kelly, showing her my phone.

"I don't know."

"Hey, B," Reese says as she walks up to us.

"Hey. Reese, who is this?" I ask, now showing her.

"Let me look in my phone…nothing."

I write back, "Yeah, standing outside."

"We'll see who shows up," I say, not thinking much of it.

I get a text back, "Cool, I'm parking now."

I look out at the parking lot, eager to identify the mystery number. My eyes land on Mark as he gets out of his car and approaches the theater. Seriously? How did he get my number? Also, why don't I have *his* number? I'm such a bad stalker.

"That was you?" I ask when he gets closer.

"Oh, my texts? Yeah, you didn't have my number?"

"No."

"I love how you didn't ask who it was," he says, laughing.

"I wanted to be surprised."

"Hey, guys," he says to the others. They smile and nod.

"All right, I vote we go in so we can save enough seats," Kelly says.

The previews haven't started yet, but the theater is already crowded. We realize the only way we are all going to sit by each other is if we sit in a middle row close to the screen. As Reese and Kelly lead the way, I make sure to be right behind Mark so that we can sit by each other. I'm no fool.

"Natalie asked me to save a seat for her next to me," Mark says as we file into the fourth row. Of course she did. Competing with one of my best friends over a guy is tough, especially when he doesn't know I like him and I don't know if he likes boys.

We're about to sit down when Mark is forced to make a choice: keep an open seat to his right between him and me, or to his left between him and Kelly. Instead of making the choice, he hovers over both seats and asks, "Where should Natalie sit?"

"Um, how about you sit here?" I say, grabbing his arm and

pulling him toward me, leaving an open seat between him and Kelly. Bold, Brendan. There's no way I was going to miss out on that opportunity.

"Excited for the movie?" Mark asks me.

"Um…nah."

He laughs. "Why not?"

"It's hard for a movie to keep my attention. I'm fine when I'm in a theater because I'm stuck here, but if I try to watch a movie at home, I'm easily distracted. And this is more of an action movie, which is not my favorite kind."

"All right, then what's your favorite mo—"

"*My Best Friend's Wedding.*"

He laughs. "Julia Roberts, right?"

"Yeah."

"Never saw it."

"It may seem like a typical romantic comedy, but it's so much more."

"What's it about?"

"Julianne—Julia Roberts—realizes she loves her best friend the day he tells her he's engaged to another woman."

"Is that the tag line from the movie poster?"

I laugh. "I'm sure it's pretty close. So then she spends the whole movie trying to get the courage to tell him how she feels."

As I explain the premise of the movie, I suddenly realize the similarities between Julianne's predicament and the situation I'm in right now. Julianne loves Michael; I like Mark. Michael loves Kim; Mark apparently likes Natalie. Julianne and I both know that the chances of Michael and Mark returning our love are slim, but we'll never know for sure unless we tell them how we feel. Unfortunately, I'm not sure if I'll ever have the courage to do that.

"All right, what's your favorite?" I ask.

"This is tough. I love *Anchorman.*"

"Oh, I actually like that one."

"Okay, good. And *Fight Club.*"

"Oh," I say, my voice dropping.

"Not a fan?"

"One of my top three least favorite movies. Turn to Kelly, though. She'll tell you how much she loves it."

"Okay, wait, let me redeem myself. *Mean Girls.*"

"Yes! There you go."

He laughs. "Too easy."

"Do you like horror movies?" I ask.

"I do, but I get *way* too scared."

"Aw, you need someone to hold you during the scary parts?"

"Exactly."

Shortly after the first preview starts, Kara appears at the left end of the row. I wave to her while she slides in next to Reese. Mark and I are still in isolation but I'm not sure for how much longer. I stop talking because I don't want to interrupt the preview, although I'd much rather continue my conversation with him.

I'm pleasantly surprised when he turns to me and whispers, "I never asked how your Thanksgiving was."

"Oh, it was pretty good. All of my sisters are still in town. It's nice to get a break from them, though."

"How many sisters do you have?"

"Five."

His eyes widen. "No brothers?"

"Nope. And they're all older."

"Five extra moms," he says.

"Pretty much. How was *your* Thanksgiving? You went to your grandparents'."

"Went to my grandparents', yeah. It was great. I'm really close with my cousins, and it was nice to see the ones who don't live near me."

"Cool."

"When's your birthday?" Mark asks.

"April fifth. Why?"

"So you're an Aries. I just think astrology is fun."

"When's yours?" I ask.

"August twenty-second."

"Oh, you're on the older side for your grade. An August birthday makes you a…Pisces?"

He laughs. "Not even close. Leo."

"Ah. So are Aries and Leo compatible?" I say before laughing like it's a joke, although I'm dead serious.

"Actually, yeah. They're a direct match."

"Makes sense why we get along so well."

"I imagine you get along with everyone."

"Well, I just try to be nice. You come off the same way."

"I try, but I'm not as open as you," he says. "You're an open book. I'm more private."

"Well, that's not bad. Although it *is* nice to be able to get things off your chest. Don't keep everything bottled up inside."

As the last preview finishes up, I turn to see Natalie climbing over our friends to get to her seat while Chris takes the open seat next to Kara. My one-on-one time with Mark is over.

During the movie, I can't help but notice how Natalie and Mark interact. Each time they turn to each other to say something, they erupt in quiet laughter. It's very cute and flirty. I'm curious how Mark would react if I were as blatant with my flirting as Natalie. In some instances, I guess I have been.

I have to admit I'm actually happy that Natalie and Mark have this connection. If they didn't, Mark would have never started hanging out with our group. I fear what would happen if they stopped liking each other.

A little less than two hours later, the movie is over. I would have liked more plot and less action, but it wasn't terrible. After the movie, we head to Applebee's for their half-priced appetizers, per usual. As I'm walking ahead of everyone else with Kara, I feel something hit me in my right shoulder blade.

I turn around and see Reese bent over with her hands in the snow, making a snowball. Kara and I quickly pack snow in our hands to create weapons for ourselves. I'm hit in the leg as I stand up and pull my arm back. I whip the snowball toward Reese but miss. Kara, however, nails her in the stomach.

"Ow!" she screams. Kara and I laugh.

Kelly and Mark join in while the others watch with disinterest. We all run around each other, trying to keep our distance while still getting close enough to make a hit. Kelly and Kara exchange blows while Reese hurls one at Mark. I'm packing up another snowball when Mark comes closer to me.

"Let's go after Reese," he says.

"Okay," I say, standing up with a snowball in hand. "One, two, three!" I throw one her way, but instead of doing the same, he turns and hits me in the side.

"What the heck!" I yell at him, shocked by his betrayal. "Oh, you play dirty." I quickly pack another snowball and throw it at him while he's bent over. It hits him in the neck. "Agh! I'm sorry! Are you okay?" He rises up with a much larger snowball, revenge in his eyes. "Crap," I say before running away.

"Yeah, you better run," he says, chasing after me.

I run into an open grassy area, now covered in white. When I look back, I see him getting closer and closer. Clearly his soccer endurance trumps my tennis endurance. I suddenly feel myself trip over something, and before I know it, I'm on my hands and knees. I feel Mark standing over me.

"All right, I give up, I give up," I say, still on the ground, covering my head with my arms but peeking at him through my fingers. He raises the snowball above me, but instead of throwing it, he drops to his knees, before collapsing on his back, breathing almost as hard as I am. I bring my arms down and roll onto my back next to him, staring up at the clear, dark sky.

"Aw, you showed mercy," I say.

"You sure about that?" Before I can react, he slams the snowball on my chest, rubbing the snow up and down my torso.

I let out a wail that turns into a laugh. "I want to punch you so hard right now."

"Whoa, I've never seen you angry," he says. "I like this side of you. Hit me, please!"

"You like me with a little edge, huh?" I sit up and go to punch him in the arm but stop before making contact.

"Oh, come on. Remember what you told me about keeping things bottled up?"

"You want me to hit you? Are you into S&M or something?" He laughs. "No, I just want you to let out your aggression. You're too nice. It scares me."

"I'm not going to punch you. Let me just shake you a little." I turn and grip both his shoulders, shaking him before returning to my back. "I feel better."

"You tried," he says, giving me two pats on my chest before rising. He reaches his hand out to help me get up.

"Oh, I'm supposed to trust you now?" I say.

"The snowball fight's over. I promise."

I reach my hand out. He grabs it and pulls me up to my feet. I wipe the snow off of my chest while he sweeps it off my back. We head back to the group that, by this time, is almost at the restaurant. Their fight seems to be over as well.

Applebee's isn't crowded, so we are immediately seated at two high-top tables pushed together near the bar. I try to sit next to Mark, but I can't arrange it without being blatantly obvious. Chris and Natalie land on each side of him. I end up diagonally across from him, but I spend most of the dinner talking with Reese and Kara, who are seated at my end of the table.

"What exactly is History Day?" I ask Reese, who has started to tell us a story about one of her school projects.

"I'll tell you what it is," she says. "One day a group of teachers thought to themselves, 'How can we give children ulcers sooner?'" Kara and I laugh. "Let's make them do a group project about anything in history. We'll keep it vague. And then let's make that project worth thirty percent of their grade for the semester."

"Oh gosh. Who's in your group?" I ask.

"Well, I was limited to the twenty-eight people in my class and each group has to have a minimum of three people, so there's me, Natalie, and Becky Phillips. Do you know who that is?" I nod. "Yeah, so I decided to get a group of really reliable, hard workers," she says sarcastically. Even though Natalie is a few seats away, I don't think she'd be offended if she heard. She's never been the most studious.

"What's the topic for your project?" Kara asks.

"We decided on communication."

"Wait, that's it?" I say. "That's a little broad, no?"

"Yeah, it is, which means I can include every piece of information I find on the phone, and the Internet, and the phonograph, and languages, and whatever else. So I dare my teacher to give me something less than an A when I turn in basically an encyclopedia."

As I keep laughing at Reese, I turn toward Mark's direction and catch him staring at me with a slight smile on his face. Once our eyes meet, he quickly looks down then back up to rejoin the conversation at his end of the table.

Toward the end of dinner, he gets up to go to the restroom.

"Is he gay?" Kelly blurts out after he leaves the table.

"Mark?" Chris asks.

"Yeah. I can't figure him out."

"Join the club," Chris says.

"He has feelings for me," Natalie says with feigned confidence. "He can't be gay."

"Or is it, 'He has feelings for you. Therefore he *has* to be gay'?" Chris says. Reese collapses in laughter.

"He's very flirty with everyone," Chris continues. "It doesn't matter if it's a girl or boy. I think he just likes the attention."

Chris's words aren't the most encouraging. I've been thinking Mark's flirtation toward me was real. I'm hoping it's not just part of his usual routine with anyone who finds him attractive.

After we get our checks and wrap up our evening, Kara asks me if I can drive her home. I didn't realize her parents dropped her off at the theater. I say my good-byes, wondering when I'll see Mark again.

I'm actually glad I have some alone time with Kara. I've noticed some tension between her and Natalie and am curious if I'm just seeing things that aren't there. I ask her about it after we get into my car.

"Oh, you're spot on with that," she tells me.

"What's the deal?"

"It's nothing new. She still thinks I put Andrew in front of my friends. I try to balance as best as I can, but I still get crap for it."

"I'm surprised because, honestly, I think you do a really good job balancing friends with a boyfriend. We still see you every weekend, and we get you alone too. It's not like you're dragging him along to all of our friend outings."

"Right? You guys never see him. The worst part is Andrew gives me crap about this too. He says I put my friends before him."

"See, now that's more true."

She laughs. "I think so too."

"Well, you and Natalie have a long history, and I'm sure the dynamic does change when a guy enters the picture. I haven't noticed a change with you and me, but it might be different with a girl-girl friendship."

"Maybe. I think it's unfair for her to punish me for having a boyfriend. I shouldn't feel guilty for hanging out with him on the weekends."

"I hear you. How is everything going with you and Andrew, by the way? I know I never ask. How long have you guys been dating now?"

"Almost a year and a half."

"Wow. How does that feel? I feel like a bad friend for not asking you this before. I think it's because I never see him. I forget he's in the picture."

"No worries. It's good. It feels...serious." I hear a shift in her voice.

"What?"

"I don't know..." By this time, I've pulled into Kara's driveway, but with her seat belt still fastened, she is showing no signs of getting out of the car.

"Clearly you're hiding something and are debating whether to tell me," I say to her. "No pressure. Obviously I won't tell anyone. You keep all of my secrets; I keep all of yours."

"Well, this might be shocking to you. It might not. Knowing you, it probably will be..."

"Okay..."

"A few months ago, Andrew and I had sex for the first time."

She's right. It *is* shocking. I feel my eyes widen. "Whoa, really?"

She nods. "This past summer. I wanted to wait until our one-year anniversary. Please don't judge me."

"I'm not, I swear."

"I know you're planning on waiting until marriage and obviously you see sex as a big deal, and I do too."

I can't blame Kara for being worried that I might judge her. I know that's an area where I need to work on myself. I need to realize that I shouldn't judge someone for doing something I wouldn't do or believing in something I don't. It's okay to have disagreements, even with your best friends.

I honestly don't judge Kara. It feels good she opened up to me about this.

"So, how do you feel about it?" I ask.

"I've had my freak-outs. I'm terrified of getting pregnant."

"Oh gosh."

"We do it very rarely."

"Andrew didn't pressure you at all…"

"No, no. Not at all. He was fine waiting as long as I wanted."

I'm fascinated that it's always the girl who decides when it's going to happen. Doesn't the guy ever want to wait, or is he ready to have sex day one? I just wish more guys saw sex as something serious and unnecessary at our age. For once, I want a guy to break the stereotype in my head. I want him to say to his girlfriend, "I'm not ready to have sex. Let's wait."

"Well, thanks for telling me," I say.

She nods. "You know I get in weird moods and all emotional."

"I love when you do. It cracks me up."

"Like when I tell you that I wake up crying for no reason? Is something wrong with me? Am I depressed?"

"I don't think so. You just overthink things."

"I know. The more I think about next year, the more stressed I get. Promise me we'll stay friends."

"Oh my gosh, are you kidding? Don't worry about us. We've been friends since first grade."

"I know, but will our group of friends stay the same?"

"I guess I'd be naïve if I said yes. I don't know. It will depend where we all end up."

Kara and I finish up our conversation before I watch her go into her house. It's crazy to think how much she and I have gone through in our friendship. We're only seventeen, but we've been there for each other our whole lives. The same goes for all of my other close friends. College may change things, but I feel lucky to have such a solid group of friends today. Friends with whom I will forever share some of my best memories.

As I drive home, my thoughts naturally shift to Mark. I relive all of the interactions I just had with him tonight: our conversations, our snowball fight, our flirting.

By the time I get home, I am filled with a happiness I've never felt before. Allowing myself to have feelings like this is so foreign to me. Yes, I had a crush on my friend, Dave, earlier in the year, but my feelings for Mark are much more intense. I feel like I've opened up a whole new door to joy and excitement.

CHAPTER FOUR

I've seen Mark at school a number of times in the past few weeks, sharing some hallway conversations with him. I've had a couple after-school meals with him and Chris too.

Also, one Saturday, Mark, Natalie, Chris, and I went to the mall for some Christmas shopping. Mark offered to drive us and picked me up first, which led to the first official time that I hung out with him alone. Granted it was only for about five minutes in his car, but it was still great.

Another night involved a bowling showdown, where Mark, Reese, and I were teamed up against the others. Reese was terrible, but we still managed to win.

I'm excited to see how it will be with him tonight when we go to Chris's to hang out.

After getting there, I'm surprised to see about ten people show up. We snack in Chris's kitchen for a little bit and then head down to the basement. Normally, I would wait to see where Mark sits down and then discreetly try to sit next to him, but this time I'm the first person to walk down the stairs, so I decide to do a little experiment.

I immediately sit down on the end of one of the couches. When Mark walks down, I see him assess the situation before proceeding to sit right next to me. He has to scoot even closer to me as more people squeeze themselves onto the couch.

Our proximity lends itself to an increase in flirting. Mark starts playing with these tiny figurine toys in his lap that belong to Chris's younger brother. He then starts touching them on my leg, walking them slowly up my thigh.

"Where are those things headed?" I ask as he moves them closer to my crotch.

"Toward something they like, apparently. I don't know. They're out of my control."

Mark turns the toys around to have them start walking back down my leg.

"What happened?" I ask. "Did they get scared?"

"Yeah, they were intimidated."

"Something big was blocking their way?"

He laughs, shaking his head. "Exactly. Too big to get past."

Immediately after that, Mark starts joking around with our friend, Beth, who is sitting on the other side of him. He places one of the toys on her arm and starts walking it up, just as he did on my leg.

"Mark, stop," Beth says. "I feel like I'm suffocating. Scoot over."

Mark turns his body toward her and places both his legs on top of hers. "Is this better?" I can tell he's in a very playful mood tonight.

Beth laughs. "I'm going to kill you." She picks up his legs and tosses them onto my lap. "There. Much better."

"Fine. I like Brendan better than you anyway," Mark says.

"I can tell. You two have a crush on each other."

I'm caught so off guard by Beth's words that I don't say anything. She doesn't even know I'm gay, let alone that I have feelings for Mark. Am I that obvious? I swear I'm subtle when it comes to my behavior around him. I'm reading too far into it; it's probably just a joke.

"Oh yeah," Mark says. "Brendan and I are dating. We didn't tell you?"

"Really? How long have you been dating?" Beth asks, playing along.

"How long has it been?" Mark asks me, his legs still in my lap.

I look at my watch. "A couple hours."

"Sounds serious," Beth says.

"Yeah, it's been moving pretty fast," Mark says.

The joking ends as he sits upright again, but it's enough to make my head spin. I've been thinking about all the times Mark flirts with me or messes around like that. The fact is he doesn't know that I'm gay. So what straight guy would repeatedly say or do these things to another supposedly straight guy? Then again, maybe he's so comfortable with his sexuality that he's fine joking around with me, knowing that it's all in good fun.

Toward the end of the night, he revives his joke one more time when no one else is listening.

"So, when are we going on our first date?" he asks.

"I'm free anytime. Just tell me when."

He smiles at me. "When was the last time you went on a date with someone?"

"I never have, really. I haven't dated anyone since sixth grade."

"What? A guy as great as you. How is that possible?"

"I guess I just haven't found someone I'm interested in."

"Who was the last person you liked?"

"Oh gosh," I say, blushing.

"Look at you. You get so uncomfortable." He grabs my shoulders and shakes them like he did the first night I met him. "Loosen up, Brendan."

"I'm in the hot seat."

"I'm just curious."

"I'll just say that hopefully I'll meet someone I click with—someone who feels the same way about me as I feel about them."

Like you, I think.

I feel that this is a perfect time to ask Mark about his ex-girlfriend, Amy, but before I have the chance to do so, Chris interrupts us.

❖

It's one week before Christmas and today is the day. And apparently Caribou Coffee shop is the place. I guess it's as good as any spot for coming out. It's actually a decision I haven't given much thought to. The timing finally feels right. And with Kara's recent revelation to me about her and Andrew, I want to be able to share something just as private with her.

With two hot chocolates sitting on the table in front of me, I try to calm my nerves as I wait for her to arrive. I know that she will be completely supportive, but it's not her reaction that I'm afraid of. It's been about nine months since I admitted to myself that I'm gay, and since then, the secret has been mine to control. But today I am releasing that secret into the world.

Staring out the window, I suddenly see Kara's tan Corolla pull into the parking lot. My heart was jogging before; now it's sprinting. I have what I'm going to say all planned out, but as I try to remember it, my brain seems to go to mush. Kara opens the door, scans the coffee shop, and sees me sitting at a small table in the back.

"Hey, what's up?" I say as she approaches the table.

"Nothing. Thanks for getting me this," she says, referring to the drink. I texted her when I got there to ask what she wanted. I didn't want to waste any more time ordering. "Here you go," she says as she hands me a five-dollar bill.

I shake my head. "My treat."

I don't want to jump right into it, especially because my pulse is unhealthily high right now, so I try as best I can to have a normal conversation with her. We talk about school and vacation plans, but we both notice an unnatural element about it all. It's finally time to tell her why I asked her here.

"All right, I told you I needed to talk to you about something." My pulse returns to its skyrocket level.

"Yes."

"Okay, well first you have to promise not to tell anyone else."

"Of course."

It's rare for either of us to be this serious, and I think it's freaking us out. There is no sarcastic humor, no smiling—just intensity.

"Okay," I continue before a long pause. "I guess I'll just say it...I'm gay."

"Wow. Okay," she says with a slight smile.

"And you're the first person I've ever told."

Her slight smile goes away, and we both return to our serious gazes. "Oh. Wow." Her reaction goes from surprise to understanding. "How long have you known? I mean, when did you...accept it?"

"In March. I actually started having feelings for Dave Nelson and, instead of suppressing them, I just let them happen."

Dave was another theater friend. We had some classes together, but we didn't become close until our high school musical junior year. Of course I never had the courage to tell him how I felt, so nothing happened. Still, he helped me accept my sexuality without even knowing it. Once I let myself feel that way for another guy, I felt free. It was exciting and exhilarating.

"Well, thanks for telling me. I'm honored to be the first one. But...are you going to tell our other friends or what?"

"I was waiting for that question. I know I have to. Well, first off, they're going to be pissed that I told you before them, but I would never have been able to tell five people at once. That's too much. Especially since I'm scared that after I tell them, it's somehow going to get back to my mom. What if they tell others? Or slip in front of their parents?"

"I hear you, but hopefully they'll know that it's not their place to tell anyone, so they'll be careful not to let it slip. But it *is* a risk. Actually, let's be real. How often do any of our parents talk to your mom?"

I laugh. "Good point. So can I tell you something else?"

"Sure."

"Well, I've developed feelings for someone over the past month...big-time."

Her forehead wrinkles as she tries to figure out who my mystery crush is. "Do I know him?"

"Mark."

"Oh my gosh. Duh! Okay, so you and Natalie are competing for the same guy. Good, good."

"Exactly." I laugh.

"Look, I know I haven't had that much contact with him, but he definitely flirts with you."

"Thank you!"

"Do you think he's gay?"

"I'll say this…I don't think he's straight. Maybe he's bi, maybe he's gay—don't know. I just feel like every time I flirt with him, he reciprocates. But even if he *is* gay, he hasn't come to terms with it yet. That's why he and Natalie have their little thing."

"Yeah, what's going on with that? It's not like they're dating. Have they even kissed?"

"Nope. I think it's kind of stalling. She told me she's getting more and more frustrated with the situation. Am I a bad friend for going after the guy she likes?"

"I don't think so. If *I* did it, I guess it would be a crappy thing to do. But since you're a guy, it's different. Wow, what a double standard."

I laugh. "Seriously."

"I mean, he either likes girls or guys," Kara continues. "So it's not really a competition between you and Natalie."

"Unless he's bisexual."

"Like Chris was bisexual a couple years ago," she says jokingly. "I have an idea. Just tell Mark you like him and see what happens."

"I love when you give me bold advice like that. You can live vicariously through me, and if it fails, there's no skin off your back."

She laughs. "True, I *do* do that. But in all honesty, you should at least consider it. If you really feel there's a chance he likes you back, it might be worth it."

"Yeah."

"I just know how safe you play things, and I get that. I do the same thing. But lately I've seen the value in taking risks and not worrying."

"For example?"

"Well, I haven't necessarily practiced what I'm preaching. Actually, here's an example…I plan to major in journalism next year and am looking for schools that have strong programs. What if I change my mind in a year, and I'm stuck at a random school that only drew me there because of my choice of major?"

"Yeah, what if that *does* happen?"

"I'll figure it out. But I can't see into the future, so I'm not going to let that worry me. I think that journalism is a good fit for me. Therefore, I'll focus on getting into the top programs for that."

"How random are some of these schools?" I ask.

"University of Missouri, University of Maryland, Syracuse."

"Okay, yeah, you've mentioned those."

"Yeah. They're schools that I would never consider if I were to major in business or something."

"Speaking of majoring in business, do you think that's a good choice for me?"

"I do. You've always been a math and science person, so I think those skills are a good fit for business, which involves accounting, and numbers, and all that."

"Yeah, I just don't know if I'd like a boring corporate job."

"Are you still considering going pre-med?" Kara asks.

"I don't want to put all my eggs in that basket, so I'm thinking I might stick with business, but then try to do all of the pre-med classes as well in case I decide to go to med school."

"You're crazy."

"I know. It would be a lot. Who knows?"

"We'll figure it out."

"You know what's cool?" I say. "You now know that I'm gay but nothing has changed. We're talking about college just like we have been all year."

"Of course nothing's changed. We're still the same people with the same friendship that we've had for years. Things won't change when you tell everyone else either."

"By the way, what did you think when I asked you to meet me today?"

"Two things. Either you're gay, or you're in love with me and thought we'd end up together, but now that I've had sex, you're done." I laugh. "I'm happy it was the former."

Well, I guess that's it. One down, plenty to go. It's a very invigorating way to start Christmas break. Now that that's out of the way, I have to mentally prepare myself for another week of family time.

CHAPTER FIVE

Major holidays like Christmas tend to evoke memories of my dad. As a result, I'm usually in a sad mood when Christmas comes—remembering what it was like before he passed away, when I was too naïve to know how great I had it. Needless to say, I was happy to get the holiday over with as fast as possible.

New Year's Eve, on the other hand, is a holiday I've always liked. It's fun to look back at the year, reliving my favorite memories and perhaps burying the ones I'd like to forget. This year has been a good one for me, filled with self-growth and so many fun times with friends.

To celebrate the stroke of midnight tonight, I will be going to a theater friend's party. I haven't seen some of my close friends since before Christmas, so I'm excited. I told Natalie that I'd stop by her place before the party to hang out.

Late in the afternoon, my phone rings, which prompts my usual delusional response: Maybe it's Mark. I'm shocked to find that today is my lucky day.

"Hello?"

"Hey, Brendan."

"What's going on?"

"Not much. You excited for the party?"

"Heck, yeah."

"Natalie mentioned that you are stopping by her place

beforehand," he says. "Do you know what time you're going? I was going to go too."

I didn't know that Natalie invited Mark as well. I guess even with the issues that they've had the past couple weeks, she hasn't given up on him.

"I was going to get there at eight-ish and then head to the party at nine," I tell him. "What are you thinking?"

"That works. Do you know what you're doing for dinner? Want to get a bite to eat before we go there?"

Holy crap. A one-on-one hang-out with Mark? I've always wanted to hang out with him alone, but I've never gotten the opportunity. And I've sure as hell never had the courage to ask him to hang out.

"For sure," I say. "Where do you want to go?"

"As if we could go anywhere but Applebee's."

I laugh. "Are you sure? I swear there are other places I like."

"Yeah, it's right by Natalie's. I can just pick you up. No need for both of us to drive tonight."

"Okay, sweet," I say. "Seven?"

"Perfect. See you then."

Wow. This night just got a whole lot more exciting. Any other time I've hung out with Mark, other people were around. Tonight is just the two of us, like a date.

A few hours later, Mark pulls into my driveway. I run out to his car like a giddy kid, but manage to compose myself before opening the passenger door.

"Hey, Mark."

"Look at that timing," he says, pointing to the dashboard clock that reads seven.

"I know. You're so prompt." I immediately notice Christmas music playing on the radio. "Christmas music still? Mark, Christmas is like three hundred and sixty days away."

He laughs. "In my book, Christmas music is acceptable for another five hours."

"All right, fair enough."

Going into the dinner, I was afraid my nerves would get the

best of me. I pictured the two of us running out of stuff to talk about ten minutes into the meal, and then realizing that my feelings for him were nothing more than a crush.

Fortunately, toward the end of dinner, the conversation and laughter are still constant. It feels so natural, and it's as if I've escaped into a secret world where it's just him and me. I can't stop smiling until he asks me something that makes my stomach drop.

"So, what do your parents do?"

He doesn't know my dad passed away, and it's always a little awkward when I have to tell someone. I decide to simply answer the question and see if the topic of my dad comes up.

"My mom doesn't work," I say. "Someone had to raise all of us kids. And my dad was a doctor."

"Cool. Wait, 'was'?" Is he retired or…?"

Crap, I thought I was in the clear. "He actually passed away when I was younger."

"Oh man, I'm sorry. I didn't know."

"No worries."

"I can't even imagine going through that."

I nod. "Yeah, it was very surreal."

"Can I ask how he passed away?"

"Heart attack."

"Gosh, so it was sudden. You didn't even have time to prepare."

I shake my head. "I don't mean to keep talking about it, but how are you doing? I know it's been years, but still…"

"I haven't been asked that question in a while," I say, trying to think of how to answer. It's touching that he cares enough to ask. "I'm good. That moment changed everything. I feel like it split my life into two parts: part one is before my dad died, part two is after. And as I get older, the two parts will get more and more disproportionate." He nods in understanding. "But you know, with that said, you've probably noticed that I'm a very happy, upbeat person, and I have a very optimistic attitude."

"I *have* noticed that," he says, smiling. "And can I say how admirable it is that you could go through something like that and remain this nice, positive person?"

"Thanks." I use the following moment of silence to change the topic of conversation. "All right, can I lighten the mood? I have a question for you."

"I'm ready…"

"What's the deal with you and Natalie?" I've been wondering how he really feels about her for the past month. I figure now that we are alone and comfortable with each other, I might as well take a shot and ask.

"What do you mean?" he says in a perfectly innocent tone.

"Do you like her or are all of her efforts futile? And I promise I won't tell her anything that you tell me."

I can tell he's debating whether to trust me or not. His answer tells me that he does. "I *did* like her, but I realized that we wouldn't be good together. Nothing against her. I know you guys are close. I think I had a crush on her, and then the more I got to know her, the more I realized we're better off as friends."

"I get it. That makes sense." I'm happy to hear that he doesn't have feelings for her, but I can't help but be bothered that he *used to*. It's my jealousy creeping in again.

"Are you going to tell her I said that?" he asks.

"No. I promise. I'm good at keeping secrets. You can tell me anything."

"Good. Speaking of Natalie," he says, looking at his watch. "It's five after eight. I know she won't be ready for us, but should we get out of here?"

"Sounds good."

As we stand and put our coats on, a crazy thought enters by mind: *Tell him. Tell Mark you like him.* The thought makes my heart and mind race as we walk to his car and I go silent. *Take a chance*, I think. *If it backfires, you'll be at Natalie's in five minutes and the awkwardness will be done.* I blame Kara for putting this in my head.

He starts his car and puts it into reverse as I put on my seat belt. This isn't going to protect me from what I might do right now.

"Oh no. Only four hours left," he says, referring to the Christmas music that's playing.

His words pull me out of my inner deliberation but, still speechless, all I can do is smile. *All right, Brendan. You're running out of time. Just decide.* The words are on the tip of my tongue. I would normally think about something like this for days or weeks before deciding what to do, but who knows when I'll be alone with him again? I deliberate for another ten seconds, hoping he doesn't find the continued silence awkward.

"Can I talk to you about something?" Oh my gosh. I decided.

"Sure," he says casually, clearly not expecting what I'm about to say. I sit in silence again. "What?" He steals a glance at me.

"Well, first off, I didn't plan what I'm about to say, so I'm sorry if it doesn't come out right."

"Okay..."

"But I guess it's pretty simple," I say, still looking forward. "Um...I...have feelings for you." I take a quick look at him before going back to my safe place of looking out at the road. His eyes are wide but still looking forward.

"Wow...I wasn't expecting that," he says.

"I'm sorry. I know that came out of nowhere. I've just really liked hanging out with you this past month and especially tonight."

"I didn't even know you were..."

"I know. No one knows I'm gay except for Kara...and now you. I can't believe I just told you." Mark doesn't say anything, so I continue to talk. "Look, if you don't feel anything for me, I understand, and you don't have to say anything right now. Once we get out of this car, we can just pretend this conversation didn't happen. I really don't want it to be awkward with us from now on. I just thought I'd take a chance. I'm normally not this spontaneous. It's just—" I decide to cut myself off. Otherwise, who knows how long my rambling will continue?

After what feels like an hour but was probably only five seconds, "Look, Brendan, I think you're really cool, and I have fun with you when we hang out, but my feelings for you are just platonic. I'm sorry."

I should have expected that, but my optimism didn't prepare for me for what I'm feeling right now. It's like a blow to the stomach and heart. I start nodding, knowing he can see me in his peripheral vision.

I feel that there's one more question I need to ask in order for me to remove any hope of our being together. "So, do you think you could ever feel anything for me?"

More silence followed by, "No. I'm sorry."

"No, no worries. I just had to ask."

"So, I assume Kara's the only one who knows how you feel about me?"

"Yep. Look, this is very new for me," I continue. "I'm not sure where we're supposed to go from here, but I really would like to be friends still. I know there might be an elephant in the room every time we hang out, but I'm willing to ignore it."

He smiles. "I think I can do that too. Like I said, I think you're really cool, and I like hanging out with you. That doesn't change."

The longest car ride ever is over as we pull up to Natalie's house. I guess that's that. It didn't go as I hoped, but I'm proud of myself. I told him how I feel. I'll never look back at this moment and kick myself for not taking a chance.

As we walk up to Natalie's front door, he brings the light-hearted atmosphere back. "All right, what are the chances she's ready?"

"Ready?" I say. "We're not heading to the party until nine, which means she probably hasn't even showered yet."

We ring the doorbell and are greeted by Natalie's dad.

"Hi, Mr. Suarez," Mark and I say.

"Hi, guys. Come on in. Natalie's in the shower."

Mark and I steal a smile at each other. We walk into the living room and have a two-on-one chat with Natalie's dad. He's very much a jokester and always tries to give me a hard time. His Spanish accent complements his upbeat personality. After we talk about my family, school, and college plans, Natalie finally walks downstairs. Of course she's not ready yet but at least she's dressed.

"Five minutes!" she says before briskly walking past us and into the downstairs bathroom with her makeup bag.

"Look at what you guys put up with," Mr. Suarez says to Mark and me as he heads into the kitchen.

"I know," I say. "I guess she's worth it."

Mark turns to me and says, "Man, you're good with parents."

"No big deal."

"Seriously, he loves you."

"He knows he can trust me. I think it's the whole 'no drinking' thing. Or maybe he knows I'm not a threat to his daughter." I give Mark a wink.

"What are you guys talking about?" Natalie yells at us from the bathroom.

"We're talking about how much longer we're going to wait here before we ditch you," I reply.

"Four minutes," she says.

"Right."

Even though Mark rejected me not even twenty minutes ago, I'm in surprisingly good spirits. I actually feel more confident and uninhibited. I think it's because I have nothing else to lose. I'm sure I haven't been a hundred percent myself around him because he made me nervous and I wanted him to like me. Now? Who cares what he thinks?

About eight—not four—minutes later, Natalie emerges from the bathroom. It's eight-forty now, so after hanging out for just a little longer at her house, we head to the party in Mark's car.

After ringing our friend's doorbell, we are greeted by her mom, who leads us down the basement. I scan the room to see who's there and immediately notice Kara, Reese, and Kelly in the corner. It's hard to miss Reese with her New Year's Eve celebratory hat. I head toward them while Mark and Natalie say hi to others.

"We need to talk later," I whisper to Kara when the others aren't paying attention. She looks at me, knowing what it must be about. It doesn't take long for Kara and me to slyly break away from the others.

To make sure Mark doesn't suspect that we're talking about him, I lay out some instructions for Kara. "All right, pretend we're talking about something normal, so whatever I say, don't act shocked or anything. And smile or laugh periodically so it looks like we're talking about something lighthearted."

"Got it," she says.

"I told you Mark and I were going to dinner tonight."

"Yes."

"Well, I was nervous how it would go, just the two of us," I say as Kara is smiling at me, following my instructions. "Well, it was perfect. I had so much fun and the chemistry was great.

"So, we're on our way to Natalie's," I continue, "and I decide to be brave and tell him how I feel about him. He was really nice about it, but he said that he only sees me as a friend." Kara loses her smile. "I know. I mean, I guess that's to be expected, but Kara, at dinner we had *so* much fun. I was flirting my butt off, and I swear he was flirting with me too."

"Oh, I believe it."

"We're too serious. Let's laugh," I instruct. We both laugh before I continue. "Everything was fine at Natalie's, but I'm just hoping I didn't mess up our friendship."

"I don't think you did. First off, he's not the type to be freaked out about that. He was probably flattered. And second, I'm sure he recognizes that that was very brave of you to tell him, especially face-to-face…in his car…where he can't escape." She and I laugh again, this time genuinely.

I'm so thankful to my friends for always making me feel better, even in sad or low points in my life. In the midst of a serious conversation, we always try to add dashes of sarcasm and humor to remind us that everything is going to be okay.

"All right, I think we've talked enough for now," I say. "Reconvene in an hour. Let's mingle with others."

The night rolls along, and I'm actually having a lot of fun. Good food and good friends have really lifted my spirits. A few minutes before the clock strikes midnight, I find myself standing with Natalie and Chris, discussing New Year's resolutions. As I do a quick scan of the room, I land on Mark. I've kind of been avoiding him the whole night, but at the same time have been busy talking with everyone else.

After we lock eyes, he raises his eyebrows and flashes his smile at me. I smile back and then look down. I'm definitely still hooked, that's for sure. To me, that smile is his way of saying that everything is okay and that nothing has to be weird. When I look back up, I see him walking my way. He slides in between Chris and me.

"Hey, guys," he says.

"Hey," we say.

"Mark, quick—what's your New Year's resolution?" Chris asks.

"Um..."

"Stop listening to Christmas music?" I say with a slight smile. He laughs and looks at me. "*That*, and hit the gym more..." As if he needs it. "And I guess be more open to trying new things."

I feel my face turn into an inquisitive stare as I scrunch my forehead, but I wipe it away by the time he looks over at me. Be more open to new things? Interesting. I can't help but wonder if he's trying to tell me something, but I let that thought escape my brain. I'm not about to get my hopes up again.

"That's...very broad, but okay," Natalie says. "Brendan, your turn."

"I want to be more brave," I say after a quick moment of reflection. I keep my gaze at Natalie but can see Mark looking at me in my peripheral vision. "I feel like I overthink things, and I'd rather take a chance and do something." Fresh off my confession to Mark, I know that one of the first things I need to do next year is tell the rest of my friends that I'm gay. The longer I wait, the more pissed they'll be that I told Kara first.

"Equally broad," Natalie says.

"The countdown is about to start," Chris says.

Our heads turn toward the TV as one year ends and another begins. I feel a sense of excitement as January first officially arrives. This new year will bring a lot of changes in my life. Soon I'll be graduating from high school, then it's off to college. Who knows where I will watch the ball drop next year? And with whom I will watch?

The stroke of midnight starts the gradual exit of the party guests. As Reese heads out, I debate whether I should go home with her so that I can avoid another potential awkward moment in Mark's car, but he and I agreed to keep things normal, so I decide to stick to the plan of riding home with him. About forty-five minutes later, he, Natalie, and I leave, saying good-bye to the handful of people who are still at the party.

As Mark turns his key in the ignition, the radio lights up, and we hear the sound of Mariah Carey's "All I Want for Christmas Is You."

"I'll change it, I'll change it," Mark says, looking at me in the rearview mirror.

"No," I reply. "This is my favorite. It can be the last one."

As I stare out the window and see the light snow falling in front of the streetlights, I let my mind absorb each of the lyrics of the song, filling me with a feeling of bitter sweetness. All *I* want for Christmas is sitting in front of me. The song ends, but I keep my gaze out the window.

"Change it now?" Mark asks. I snap back into reality and nod to him in the mirror.

After we drop off Natalie, I move to the front seat and close the door. Here we are again. I decide that I will absolutely not bring "us" up on the car ride home. There's no point, and nothing else needs to be said.

"You have fun tonight?" I immediately ask. I try to keep my voice upbeat so as not to make him think I'm upset about our earlier conversation. I can't fault him for being honest with me, and I don't want him to feel bad about it.

"Yeah, I did. You?"

"A lot of fun, yeah." After some silence, I add, "Only a couple more days left of freedom."

"I know. Monday will be a rude awakening."

More silence, but at least the radio is on to defuse it. I try to think of something—*anything*—to say, but I'm stumped. The car ride is short, so before I know it, Mark is turning onto my street. He ends the silence this time.

"Well, enjoy the rest of your break, Brendan."

"Thanks, you too. Thanks for driving."

"Yeah, no problem. I'm sure I'll see you next week at school."

"Sounds good," I say as he pulls into my driveway. "Later."

I step out of the car and head inside my house. I'm not tired at all, but after saying a quick hello to my dogs sleeping in the laundry room, I go to bed.

CHAPTER SIX

I wake up the next day with three text messages: one from Kara asking me to call her when I wake up to give her more details about the night before, one from Natalie saying that she's over Mark because she doesn't think he's into her, and one from Mark. My normal reaction when I see a text from Mark is excitement, and while I get some of that, this time I'm more curious what it says than anything else.

His text reads, "Hey Brendan, I don't know how I came across last night, and I just want you to know that I'm flattered by what you told me. I'm sure it wasn't easy, and I'm happy that you were willing to share that with me."

I stare at the text but have no reaction. It's a sweet gesture and shows that he really does want to remain friends, but either my sleep or the new year has given me clarity. I'm not going to get my hopes up over this. I don't want to talk about it with him anymore. Maybe I even need some distance to get over him. Without much thinking, I craft a response: "Thanks Mark. I'm glad it's off my chest and we're still cool." Short, to the point, and honest.

After brushing my teeth and getting dressed, I shut my bedroom door and call Natalie to get more details about her text.

"Hello?" she says in a full voice.

"Whoa, you're up? I was ready to leave a funny voicemail."

"Yeah, remember my family comes over every year on New Year's Day? I'm getting ready for that."

"Oh yeah. Can you talk? I got your text."

"Ugh, yes. Okay, first off, I haven't had that much hope these past couple weeks with Mark because he is just so hot and cold."

"Okay, Katy Perry."

"I *knew* you were going to reference her."

I laugh. "Sorry, go on."

"So last night, it was more of the same. I barely spoke to him. And when you guys were at my house, I didn't feel any romantic vibes whatsoever. I feel like *I'm* the one pursuing; it's completely one-sided. We've been hanging out for over a month now, and there's been no progress."

It's so hard not to share with her *my* New Year's Eve experience with Mark. That's okay; I probably shouldn't dwell on it anyway.

"So, do you not want to hang out with him anymore?" I ask. "Will he no longer be invited out with us?" I'm anxious to hear her answer. I know it would be easier for her and me if we stopped seeing Mark altogether, but it's hard to imagine that.

"I don't know," she says. "I'm not that devastated because it wasn't like a legit relationship. More like a crush that has lasted too long."

"Right."

"And Chris was friends with him long before I met him, so I wouldn't stop him from inviting Mark somewhere. *I'm* just not going to do it."

"Yeah, that makes sense."

"Hold on," she yells to her mom or dad in the background. "Sorry, I should get back to preparing for this party, but text me if you want to stop by later."

"Okay, cool. Bye!"

I eat some breakfast and finish my third task of the day by calling Kara to give her a rundown of last night in more detail.

"So, you're okay?" she asks after I finish unleashing on her.

"I am."

"Good. Well, I'm sure you'll feel better as time goes on."

"Agreed. So I was thinking," I continue, "and I think I need to tell everyone else I'm gay ASAP."

"Yeah, I think so too. New year..."

"New year, new me," I say in a sarcastically energetic voice. "Should I try to do it this weekend? I know Kelly is out of town next weekend and I really want to do it all at once with everyone there."

"Dinner tomorrow night?" Kara asks.

"Why not? I could try to arrange it. I just want to get it over with."

"Let's do it. I'm sure everyone is free."

I spend the rest of the day making calls to my closest friends, trying to act as casual as possible about this "coming out" dinner. Reese, Kelly, and Chris are all confirmed. The only one left is Natalie. I wait until nighttime to call her so that I don't interrupt her family party.

"Can I bring Billy?" Natalie asks. "He came to the party today and mentioned hanging out tomorrow." Her neighbor joins us in our outings once in a blue moon. Of course tomorrow night is the night she wants to hang out with him.

"Um, let's just have it be the six of us," I say in the nicest way possible.

"Wha—seriously?"

"Yeah. You'll see why."

"What do you mean?"

"It's a surprise. Just trust me." Oh good. Now I'm painting my coming out as a fun event that will thrill her.

"You're so weird. Fine," she says, giving up.

❖

The next day, I'm surprised to find I'm not really nervous about tonight. I feel very fortunate to have a group of friends I know will accept me for who I am. Some might expect a place like Ohio to have people who are very closed-minded and not accepting of others' differences. I know that may be true in some parts of the state but where I live, I think people are pretty accepting—at least people *my* age.

I've gotten a taste of what it's like to tell someone I'm gay with

Kara and even Mark. Each time I do it, the weight on my shoulders gets a little lighter. After tonight, I'll feel as light as a feather.

Forget what I said about not being nervous. By the time my friends and I sit down at dinner, I am a wreck but am trying my hardest not to show it. Based on my experience when I told Kara, I should have expected to feel this way.

I decide to tell them after we order our dinners. You know, so they can lose their appetites right before the food arrives. I'm sitting on the inside up against the wall with Kara to my right and Natalie directly across from me. I take a deep breath and begin.

"Hey guys, can I talk to you about something?"

"Is this where the surprise comes in?" Natalie asks.

I try to laugh. "Yeah, I'd say so. Okay, I told Kara something recently, and I want to share it with you guys as well. But after I do, please don't tell anyone." I scan the table and see them all staring intensely back at me. Chris has an ever-so-slight smile on his face, perhaps knowing what I'm about to say. "You promise?" I ask them.

They nod in agreement. The silence continues as I fail to get any words out. I turn to look at Kara and find her staring at me expressionless.

"Okay, you're freaking me out now," Natalie says. "Is it bad?"

"No."

"It's okay, Brendan," Reese says. "Just say it."

"Okay. I'm gay." I lift my head up to see a mixed bag of reactions: Kelly's eyes are wide, Reese's nod indicates she's not too surprised, and Natalie looks like she'll burst into laughter at any moment.

Chris breaks the silence. "Ugh! Yes!"

"I'm guessing that's not a surprise to you," I say to him.

"Wait, you knew?" Natalie asks Kara.

"I told her literally a couple of weeks ago," I say before Kara can answer. "I needed to tell someone and couldn't handle coming out to everyone all at once yet." The answer seems to go over fairly well, but I get a sense that Natalie and Kelly are a little annoyed.

"How do you feel?" Reese asks.

"Um, I feel good but am still trying to gauge your reactions. It's nice to finally get it over with. What are you guys thinking?"

"I hope this isn't offensive, but I mean, you're obsessed with Kelly Clarkson," Reese says. I laugh as she continues. "So, we've all thought about it at one point or another, but I wasn't sure."

Natalie chimes in. "Yeah, I'm not surprised that you're gay, but I just wasn't expecting this tonight."

"Kelly?" I say. She hasn't said anything yet and seems to be the most surprised.

"Um, yeah, similar to what they said. I've thought about it too, but last year, I started to doubt myself because you hadn't come out yet. And with our group of friends, I figured if you really were gay, you would have told us by now."

"Well, it took me a little while to accept it. It wasn't until March of last year."

"Do you have a crush on Mark?" Reese blurts out.

I laugh. "You're good. Yes, I do."

"So you and I have been competing for the same guy," Natalie says.

"Exactly," I say. "And apparently neither one of us is winning."

She shakes her head. "I guess he's asexual because if he doesn't want *us*…"

I laugh. "I know, right?"

"So, who else knows?" Kelly asks.

"No one." *Well, Mark*, I think, but I don't need to go into that right now.

Kelly continues her questioning. "Are you going to tell your mom?"

"No. I mean, eventually, but I can't handle that right now. That's why you guys can't tell anyone."

"I have a question," Reese says. "Are there any guys who are out at your school?" Chris clears his throat. "Besides Chris, sorry."

"Yeah," Chris answers before rattling off a few names.

"Are people nice to them?" Reese asks.

"I think so," I say. "Our school environment has gotten a lot better over the past few years. When I was a freshman, a kid in my grade called me to tell me that he was leaving the school because he was made fun of for being gay."

"Aw, that's horrible." Kelly says. "Wait, why did he call you?"

"He wanted to thank me for being nice to him. We had a lot of classes together."

"So, how is it different now?" Reese asks.

"I think the school made a conscious effort to change the atmosphere," I say. "We did the play *The Laramie Project* at school this year."

"The *only* play of yours I ever missed," Reese says.

"That's right. Well, the play revolves around the story of a kid who was killed for being gay. There's no way Xavier would have done that my freshman year."

"You're probably right," Chris says. "But there are still some guys who are completely homophobic. Some of the stuff I hear…"

"Yeah. I guess that's the case at any school as big as ours. I mean, it's over a thousand teenage boys. Why do you ask, Reese? Just curious?"

"Yeah, just curious what it would be like for a gay guy at an all-guys school. Or if a girl came out at our school."

"Girls at our school wouldn't care," Natalie says. "They're too into themselves to care about other people. Anyway, do you guys like my hair like this?"

We all laugh. Everything is just as it was before the dinner started. Going home, I feel a huge sense of relief. All of my close friends know, and nothing has changed. Christmas break has been a little crazy, but I'm glad that it has ended this way.

CHAPTER SEVEN

The first week back from break is rough. Final exams are coming up, so that has added to my stress. I'm not sure why I loaded up on so many tough classes this year: AP French Literature, AP English Literature, AP Government, Honors Geometry II, Physics, and Theology. At least I have Chorus fourth period to give me a little break.

I guess I shouldn't worry too much about how I do considering most of the colleges to which I've applied have already given me their decisions. I received a decision letter from Boston College on Tuesday and it's a yes. Schools must have mailed out a chunk of decisions on the first business day of the new year because Boston College's letter was coupled with a rejection from Columbia. Not too shocking. That means the only school I'm waiting on now is Notre Dame, but honestly I don't think it will matter what they say. It's too rural. I want to be in a city.

I go the first three days of the week without seeing Mark at school. Detoxing from him feels good. I need a little separation to help me move on. *Then* maybe he and I can continue our friendship. On Thursday, my detox ends.

After my last class of the day, I walk into the courtyard area of my school and see him standing by a bench, chatting with Chris. I normally just meet Chris at my car but when I spot them, I decide to stop and talk. Any hopes I had of getting over him quickly were extinguished about one minute into the conversation.

"Chris told me about Boston College," Mark says. "Congrats."

"Oh, thanks. Yeah, I'm excited."

"I'd prefer you a little closer," Chris says, "so that I don't go totally crazy during my senior year here, but whatever."

"I still might end up at Ohio State. That's close enough for weekend trips. And Reese and Kelly will be there." He doesn't seem satisfied. "And you'll still have Mark here."

"Yeah, and I'm all for taking road trips to visit Brendan," Mark tells Chris before smiling at me. Yep, definitely not over him.

"Yeah, Boston's only a…nine-hour drive?" I say.

"Ugh," Chris says. "Just keep me in mind when you make your decision."

"Of course."

During our conversation, my former crush, Dave Nelson, walks up and joins us. He and Chris start talking about something, but Mark and I are clearly on the outside of the conversation. I don't mind; I just continue to stare at them to avoid Mark.

"So how's your week going?" Mark quietly asks me after a few seconds of silence.

I reluctantly turn to him. "I'm getting there. How about you?"

"Not bad."

"Any soccer games this week?"

"Yeah, I have one on Saturday on the east side."

"Where on the east side?"

"Brendan, you know you won't know where it is. It's outside of your bubble."

I can't contain my smile, the same smile I always get when he teases me. "Try me."

"Gates Mills."

"You made that up."

He laughs. "I prove my point."

"I should know these places. I used to travel every weekend for tennis tournaments."

"Well, you'll have to come to one of my games sometime. It

will get you more familiar with cities that are outside of a ten-mile radius of your house."

"Only if you come to one of my tennis matches."

"Only if you play tennis with me sometime, remember?"

Why can't he like me? We get along so well. This is torture. Chris finishes talking to Dave and asks if I'm ready to go. I want to continue to talk to Mark, but instead I say good-bye.

❖

The next day, after getting home from school, I devote some time to studying. Finals begin on Monday, so I need to take advantage of all the free time I have this weekend.

Fortunately, I'm still able to squeeze in some time with friends. Tonight we are going to my high school's basketball game. Kara was going to hang out with her boyfriend, but Natalie guilted her into coming with us, so our entire crew of friends will be there. Over the past month, so much of my attention has been on Mark. I'm happy to not have to worry about that tonight. Before I know it, my friends and I will be off to college. I need to take advantage of the time we still have with each other.

A couple hours later, as I'm wrapping up my studying, my phone rings. It's Mark. Holy crap. Other than yesterday at school, I haven't talked to him since New Year's. I have to let it ring three times before I can catch my breath.

"Hello?" I say.

"Hey, Brendan."

"What's up?"

"Nothing, you?"

"Just studying," I say as casually as I can manage.

"Nice. How was your week?"

Where is this going? It can't just be a call to catch up, right?

"Kind of brutal," I respond. "I'll be glad when next week is over."

"I know, I hear you."

Silence. I throw my arm in the air, waiting for this conversation to go somewhere, but I'm not going to guide it. I want to wait and see where he takes it.

"Are you going to the game tonight?" he continues.

"Yeah, are you?"

"Yep." I guess Chris invited him.

"Cool. Should be fun."

Silence again. Okay, was *that* the point of his calling? To see if I'm going to the game?

"I have another question," he says.

"Go for it."

"How's your New Year's resolution coming along?"

It takes me a couple of seconds to remember our conversation with Chris and Natalie at the New Year's party.

"Oh, about being more brave?" I ask. "Actually, it's going really well so far. How about yours? Open to new things?" I say in a joking tone, remembering his resolution.

"Well, that's why I'm calling you." More silence as my brain spins. I head upstairs to my room to get privacy. "I've been thinking a lot about our conversation on New Year's," he continues, "and honestly, I've been thinking a lot about you." I stop halfway up the stairs. "Are you there?"

I nod before saying, "Yes."

I quickly climb the remaining steps and speed walk to my room, shutting the door behind me. My adrenaline is pumping too hard for me to sit down, so I pace back and forth across my room.

"Well, I've been trying to sort out my thoughts this past week," he says, "and I'm still confused and trying to figure it all out, but what I do know is that I have so much fun when I hang out with you. And also, I'm really attracted to you." His voice gets quiet as he finishes his declaration.

"Wow," I say, eyebrows raised.

"Yeah."

"Holy crap." I start to smile as it hits me. He is telling me exactly what I've wanted to hear for the past six weeks.

He laughs. "My thoughts exactly. Tell me what you're thinking."

"What made you…? Or…what…?" I can't find the right question to ask. Fortunately, he knows what I'm trying to say.

"When we were in my car on New Year's, and I was telling you I just saw you as a friend, I kept hearing this voice in my head that told me I was lying. Ever since I met you, I've wanted to impress you so that you like me. I would get nervous around you. I would look forward to seeing you. Feelings that I've previously had for girls, I was starting to have for you. I'm still a little freaked out, if I'm being honest. I don't know what this means in terms of my sexuality, but I decided to take a chance and see what happens."

"That's okay if you don't know," I reassure him. "It's about following your feelings, and you've done that."

"That's what I think too. See, we're always on the same page."

"Now that the shock has worn off, I can tell you that I am so happy right now."

"I'm glad to hear that because I was worried it was too late."

"Oh, heck no. So now what? The scenario in my head never played out this far with you."

"Well, I think it's about time we had a proper date. I know we have the game tonight, so can you hang out tomorrow night?"

"In the middle of finals? Absolutely."

He laughs. "Awesome. And look, I know that you've been keeping Kara in the loop on all of this, but is it okay if we keep this conversation between us? I'm just still paranoid about everything."

I knew that was coming. "I understand completely. My lips are sealed, I promise." *It's going to be hard as hell*, I think, but my lips are sealed.

"Cool. Well until tonight, Brendan."

"All right, Mark. See you in a couple hours."

"Can't wait."

I stop pacing and stand with my phone in my right hand, held to my chest. Did that just happen? I fall back onto my bed and stare at the ceiling for a minute, letting it all sink in. This is the point where I would normally call Kara to spill all the details. But keeping this news to myself feels right.

I hear a knock at my door. "Brendan?" It's my mom.

"Yeah?"

"What are you doing?" she asks, now opening the door.

"Nothing, I just got off the phone."

"Who were you talking to?"

This is foreign to me, but I have to lie to her. "Reese," I say, randomly picking one of my friends.

"All right, well, clean up your room. It's a mess."

I put on my iPod and blast the happiest music I have while dancing and cleaning. I keep reliving the last five minutes of my life over and over. This is amazing.

As my mind wanders, I realize that tonight's going to be tricky. I want to talk to Mark as much as possible, but now that my friends know I have feelings for him, they will be a lot more conscious of my interactions with him. And let's not forget about Kara, who thinks that I'm trying to get over him after being turned down. What will she think if I'm acting chummy with him the whole night?

I have to make a conscious effort to not be so obvious tonight. Well, not just tonight, but anytime I hang out with him in a group. This might be tougher than I thought. I need my friends to gradually see me getting more comfortable around him each time we hang out, as if I have gotten over him and am now able to just be friends with him.

❖

I want to ride to the game with Mark, but that wouldn't work with my whole "don't be obvious" plan. Plus I already told Kara I'd give her a ride. She and I get to my school a little before seven, expecting to be the first ones there. After paying for our tickets, we find that we're wrong. Reese and Kelly are already inside, sitting in the third row close to the door.

We wait for the current play to be over before scurrying toward the bleacher seats that they saved for us. I immediately notice Kelly's new hairstyle.

"Whoa, someone has a new 'do," I say.

"Yes, I got bangs. I'll probably regret it in a week."

"Very trendy," Kara says. "I like it."

"How was your week, B?" Reese asks.

"Long. I have finals next week. When do you guys have yours?"

"Next week," Kelly says.

"At least we're in it together. Does that mean your History Day project is due too?"

"Yep," Reese says. "Did I break away from my group so that I could do a solo project? Yep."

I laugh. "What? I thought you have to have at least three people in your group."

"I talked to my teacher and explained that it wasn't working with Natalie and Becky."

"Is Natalie pissed?" Kara asks.

"I don't care. And no, she's not. She's oblivious. So I'm looking forward to next week," Reese says in a sarcastic tone. "And after tonight, I'll be cooped up all weekend studying."

"Same," I say. *You know, other than my first date tomorrow night with Mark*, I think. At least everyone will be busy so I don't have to come up with an excuse as to why I can't hang out.

About ten minutes later, Natalie and Chris show up and file in next to us. Come on, Mark, get here already.

"Guess who we just saw," Natalie says to me. "Mr. Fukuda." He's the director of our musical this coming year. He rotates directorship every year with another teacher at our school. When he directed us two years ago, he put Natalie and me in the chorus. Hopefully this year, he'll see us as lead potential.

"Did you give him an impromptu preview of your audition?" I ask.

"Maybe if I knew what song I'm going to do."

"I hear you. We have a week and a half to figure it out."

As I'm talking to Natalie, I'm the first one to spot Mark walking into the auditorium. He flashes me a smile and a wink.

After saying hi to us, he sits down on the end next to Chris. While the two of them chat, Reese starts to talk to me about something, but I can't snap out of my distraction, knowing Mark is just a few seats away from me.

"What would *you* do?" she asks me.

"Um…wait, repeat what you said. I got sucked into the game for a second." Yeah, sure, the game.

"I could live with Abby next year and know what I'm getting into, or I could go with a random roommate and risk hating her."

I can't believe we're already talking about her college living situation. It's probably going to be months until I pick a *school*, let alone a roommate. Reese and Kelly have had their eyes set on Ohio State for a while now, so once they got accepted, it was a no-brainer for them.

"Well, you're not really close to Abby, right?" I ask. "So it would be like living with an acquaintance that you trust. You know she's nice and responsible and all that."

"Right. And even if living with her doesn't go as well as I hoped, it's not like a friendship would be ruined because we're not close friends."

"Whereas if you lived with Kelly—"

"We'd kill each other by the end of the year," Reese says.

"I think living with Abby is a good option, but honestly, I would still suggest living with someone random. You would hopefully become friends, and then you'd meet even more people through her."

"But I think I would be able to meet people through so many other ways. I wouldn't need to rely on my roommate and her social circle."

"True. You know what?" I say.

"What?"

"I can tell you already made up your mind."

"I think you're right."

"So, go for it. It's one less thing to worry about over the next seven months."

"Now I can spend all my time trying to convince you to choose Ohio State."

"We'll see. I'm hungry. Do you guys want food?" I ask Reese and Kelly.

"Yeah, can you get me a Diet Coke?" Kelly says. "Screw it. I'll have nachos too. I have money."

"South Beach Diet is over?" I ask her.

"All bets are off during finals week."

"Anyone else want food?" I ask as I cross in front of everyone.

"Yeah, I'll come with you," Mark says.

"You read my mind," I say to him as we walk toward the concession stand.

"I had to take that opportunity to get some alone time with you. How are you?"

"Good. It wasn't a prank? That was really you on the phone today?"

"It was all real," he says as we get in line for food. "All right, what are we getting?"

"I'm starving. I could eat a lot."

"Me, too. I say cheese fries, for sure."

"Yes. A couple soft pretzels."

"Hot dogs?" he asks, still looking at the menu.

"Perfect. Can you handle the foot-long or you just want a six-incher?"

"You're so bad," he says, nudging me with his elbow.

"It's an innocent question."

"Not coming from you, it isn't. I know you." He turns to me and leans in. "To answer your question, I can handle the foot-long." His words send a shiver up my body.

"I wish I could have seen your face when we talked on the phone today," he continues.

"Let me reenact it for you." I turn to him with my eyebrows raised and my mouth wide open.

He laughs. "That shocked?"

"Yes. Usually stuff like this doesn't work out. I can't believe it."

We get our food and show up at the end of our row with our hands full. Before Natalie and Chris stand up to let me past, I debate whether to just sit on the end with Mark. I know it's too obvious, so I head back to my original seat instead.

"So, it looks like you and Mark are okay?" Kara quietly asks me after I sit down.

"Yeah, we're good," I say casually. "We've seen each other at school this past week and talked. I mean, what can I do? I have feelings for a straight guy."

"I guess that makes it easier for you to move on, knowing you can't do anything about it."

"Exactly."

"Okay, I'm bored," Chris says loudly.

"It's not even halftime," Kara says.

"Let's play the question game," Chris says.

"What's that?" Reese asks.

"Someone asks a question, and we all have to answer it," he explains.

"This is Chris's way of asking us who our same-sex crushes are," I say.

"Oh, gosh," Kelly says. "This crap again? Let's start with an easier question, like something we're afraid of or something."

"Okay, Mrs. Silverstone, I'll go first," I say. "I'm afraid of... fear." My friends laugh.

"You're so weird," Natalie says before continuing with, "Let's all go around the room and say something we love. I'll go first. I love..."

"Love," she and I say in unison.

"Let's all go around the room and say something we hate," Chris says. "I hate...basketball."

We all laugh before Kelly looks at Chris and says, "I hate Debbie Downers."

"Really?" Chris says. "I hate bangs."

Kelly tries to maintain a serious face but cracks and starts laughing. "Touché."

By the start of the fourth quarter, with finals almost upon us, we all decide to call it a night.

"See you, Mark," I say. He extends his arms to give me a hug. "See you tomorrow," he whispers to me while we're embracing. I try my hardest not to smile but I can't help it. Fortunately, no one is looking at me.

CHAPTER EIGHT

Considering I've been dreaming about it since the day I met him, I decide to take the lead in planning my first date with Mark. I pick a local Italian restaurant near his house for dinner, followed by a late movie. His parents are much less suspicious than my mom, so when he tells them that his friend, Brendan, will be driving him tonight, they don't think twice about it.

I pull into his driveway, nervous but mostly excited about seeing him. A few seconds later, he walks out of his front door with a huge smile on his face. He looks unbelievably cute.

"Hi, buddy," he says, after getting inside.

"Hi. How are you?"

"Good. Finally we're alone together."

"I know. It was hard to restrain myself last night."

"So, where are you taking me?"

"Well, I know your favorite food is Italian, and I remember you telling me about a certain restaurant you went to for your birthday last year."

"No way," he says. "Cipriano's?"

"You got it."

"I can't believe you remembered that."

"Oh, it took a lot of Googling. I knew it started with a C, but that's about it."

"I'm excited."

I hold the restaurant door open for Mark as we walk inside the small, dimly lit space. The darker the better, so that no one sees us. Italian music plays at a low volume while we take our seats at a table for two.

"So, here we are," I say.

"Gosh, you look…you look really good."

My smile can't get any wider. "Thanks, Mark. You look very cute yourself."

I've never been able to say something like that to another guy. For weeks I have been wanting to tell Mark how cute I think he is.

"Is it weird that I'm nervous?" he asks.

"I am too. We shouldn't be. It's not like this is the first time we've hung out."

"Exactly."

"Although the last time we went to dinner together, it didn't end quite as I had hoped."

He laughs. "Tonight will be different, I promise."

"So how was your day? Didn't you have soccer?"

"I did."

"Did you win?"

"Duh."

I laugh. "Did you score?"

His face changes. "Okay, no, but—"

"Uh-huh."

"*But* I had two assists," he quickly says.

"Nice. So, where do you usually play, or is it all over?"

"Well, this game is for the travel league I'm on, so we play all over the place, but still in the Cleveland area. Sometimes Columbus."

"Gotcha."

"When does tennis season start for you?" he asks.

"Early April. Practices start in March, I think, but I'll still be doing the musical then so I'm able to skip them. You know I have auditions for that in a couple weeks, right?"

"Oh yeah, that's right. Are you going to get the lead?"

"Duh."

He laughs.

"Actually, I don't know," I say. "I hope so. The part I'm going for is a little high for my vocal range."

"You know, I've never heard you sing before."

"And we're going to keep it that way for a long time."

After ordering our food, I become less nervous, and my conversation with Mark is as natural as ever.

"I have a question," I say.

"I love when you set up your questions."

"I was thinking about this yesterday. For the past couple months, you've been hanging out with me and my group of friends a lot. So who else do you hang out with? I don't even know who your closest friends are."

"Well, I have my soccer friends and people from school, but I don't usually hang out with them on the weekends," he explains. "My family is Croatian, and it's a really tight-knit community here, so I actually spend a lot of time with them. Like, my cousins and stuff."

"Oh yeah, I remember Natalie talking about this. So were your parents born in Croatia?"

"Yep."

"Do you speak Croatian fluently? That's the name of the language, right?"

He laughs. "Yes and yes."

"Cool. I didn't know that. I just know you taught Chris how to say some dirty things in Croatian."

"At his request."

"Naturally. What's the phrase that he always says?"

"I'm not telling you. It will turn me on too much if you say it to me."

"But it might come in handy someday," I say. His smile fades. "I'm kidding. Sorry, inappropriate first date discussion."

He snaps out of his blank stare. "Sorry, I was letting my mind go to bad places."

"Oh, phew! I thought I offended you."

"Hell no," he says. "But we should switch subjects before I get any more excited."

"Hold on. Now *my* mind is going to bad places."

I've never even kissed a guy before, so my hormones are racing when I picture myself going even farther with Mark. Of course I'm not ready to do anything sexual with him yet, but it's sure nice to fantasize about it.

He snaps us back into a safe conversation. "Okay, back to our friendship discussion. I've met all of your close friends, right?"

"Yeah, pretty much. I have a couple other friends from grade school who I'm close with, but I don't see them that often because we have separate groups of friends."

"That's cool you've known all of your friends for so long."

"It *is*. I grew up with them, so I've always been myself around them without even thinking about it. If you haven't noticed already, I'm kind of a weird guy. They understand that and appreciate it."

"So, are you close to your family?" he asks.

"Not really. Maybe as I get older I will be. There are some pretty significant age gaps between my sisters and me that won't seem as big when I'm in my twenties."

"Makes sense. My sister's only a year younger than me, and we definitely have our issues."

Our waitress interrupts our conversation, placing our food on the table. "Here you go, guys. Enjoy."

"Thanks," Mark and I say in unison.

"So, can I be honest about something?" Mark asks. I nod. "Last night at the game…keeping my distance from you was a lot harder than I thought it would be."

"I know."

"And I could tell Natalie wasn't too happy I was there. It might be easier if I don't hang out with the group as much, at least for now."

"I understand. I think it's hard when Chris and Natalie are there because they know you better than everyone else and are more aware of your actions. Reese or Kelly or whoever else wouldn't think twice because you're just an acquaintance."

"Right. I agree."

"This is a good time to bring up something that I was going to tell you tonight," I say. "Remember a week ago when Kara was the only one who knew that I'm gay?"

"Yeah."

"Well, that's not the case anymore. I told everyone else last week."

"Whoa, seriously?"

"Yeah. I knew I was going to do it soon, and I decided that last weekend was as good as time as any."

"So, how'd it go?"

"It was good. I'm so happy that they all know now. No more secrets. Oh wait…"

"Sorry."

"I'm kidding. It's worth it. But you need to know that I told them I like you. At this point, I had no hope that something was going to happen with us."

"Okay," he says, "but they don't know about anything that happened this week."

"Right. And Kara's actually the only one who knows about New Year's. I didn't tell anyone else."

"Okay."

Mark and I finish our dinner and head to the movie theater. On the way, he asks me what movie we are seeing.

"Well, let's just say that you might need me to hold you during it," I tell him.

"It's a horror film?" I nod. "You know you don't need a scary movie to get me into your arms."

I pick up our tickets, and we head to the food line. "Popcorn or snacks?" I ask.

"Snacks."

"That's what I was thinking. Okay, what kind? Let's say what we want on three. If it's the same thing, we're too good."

"Okay, let me think," he says. "Okay, one, two, three. Sour Patch Kids."

"Sno-Caps." I laugh. "Fail. I guess we're getting both."

During the film I'm distracted because I'm trying to muster up the courage to hold Mark's hand. I worry about how comfortable my arm will be after I do it, or if the hand holding will get old after a minute, or if he wants both hands free to eat the candy. I feel like I'm in eighth grade or something.

I finally reach my right arm over the armrest and grab his left hand. He looks at me and smiles before starting to lightly rub his thumb on the back of my hand. I can't believe how much excitement I get from simply holding his hand. We naturally adjust our hand placements throughout the movie. At each scary part, he grips my hand tighter.

On the way home, seemingly without thinking, I put my hand on his thigh, drumming my fingers to the beat of the song on the radio.

"Did you have fun?" I ask.

"So much fun. I'd say date one was a huge success."

"Well, we'll have to try to top it next time."

"I'm in charge of planning date number two," he says.

"Perfect."

I pull into his driveway, and my nerves instantly return. It's time for the good-bye. I can't initiate the first kiss. First off, I've never kissed a guy before. And as for the last time I kissed a girl, it was two years ago during a game of Truth or Dare. That doesn't count.

"Thanks for everything, Brendan."

"Of course."

"We have to figure out a time to hang out this week, in spite of finals madness."

"For sure. Lunch or something."

"But our official second date will be next weekend."

Mark and I stare into each other's eyes for a couple of seconds, smiling. I don't even know if I want him to kiss me right now. I am way too nervous and need more preparation or something. Instead of a kiss, he raises his arms and leans in for a hug. We embrace tightly for a few seconds before letting go. It's a perfect good-bye.

"Good night, Brendan."

"Night, Mark."

My smile remains on my face as I watch him walk up his driveway and into his house. Once I know that he is safe and sound inside, I reverse my car and head home.

CHAPTER NINE

The next day I wake up, ready for a long day of studying. After my amazing night with Mark, even prepping for six finals can't bring me down. Fortunately, I only have one final Monday morning and can spend the rest of the day studying.

I feel prepared for my first final, French Lit, but I do a little extra cramming Monday morning before heading to school. I'm glad this one is first because it's going to be awful, and I want to get it out of the way. I'm not big into literature in general. My short attention span for movies translates to books as well. Taking tests about English literature is hard enough for me. *French* literature? Forget it.

The final consists of four essay questions. First question: *In Voltaire's* Candide, *discuss the portrayal of religious figures.* Seriously? I'm supposed to write my answer in French? I'm not going to lie; I didn't even read the French version of this novel. I wanted to have some comprehension of the story so I read the English translation. The next ninety minutes should be interesting. Fortunately, this class has a big curve. I sure as heck won't get a five on the AP test at the end of the year but I might manage to pull off an A in the class.

Tuesday brings Government (pretty easy) and Geometry (moderately difficult). Halfway there. Wednesday is my English Lit and Physics finals. English was a lot easier than I expected. As for

Physics? Well, it's actually my favorite class, so I found it pretty easy and straightforward. What can I say? I'm a math and science guy.

Now all that separates me from a three-day weekend is my Theology final tomorrow. An hour or so of studying should suffice. Mark and I are planning to get lunch after our last finals. Talk about motivation to finish my test as soon as possible.

And that's exactly what I do. To celebrate our freedom, Mark and I decide to go to a French café near our school. I've never been to the restaurant before, but a chocolate crêpe sounds delicious.

We meet in the courtyard of our school and walk to the restaurant. It's the first time I've seen him since our date five days earlier. I can't contain my smile at the sight of him. He's wearing tight khaki pants that accentuate his round, perky butt and a baby blue dress shirt that make his eyes look bluer than ever. How does he look this good in a school uniform?

The restaurant isn't crowded at all. I guess we're a little early for the lunch rush. Or maybe it never really gets crowded. Mark and I are seated away from the other patrons, as if the hostess knows that we prefer being secluded.

We start by exchanging recaps of our finals and predicting our grades.

"So, you're saying I shouldn't take AP French next year," Mark says.

"Gosh, no!"

"Mr. Trumble keeps telling me I should."

"Well, I'm sure Chris will take it, so it could be fun. It's just hard."

"Can I tell you something that concerns me about you?" Mark says as I'm chowing down on my crêpes.

"Yes. I'm scared."

"Your diet…is terrible."

I laugh. "I'm a picky eater."

"I don't think I've ever seen you put a vegetable in your mouth."

"Because they're gross."

"What?!"

"They just don't taste good. I'd rather have chicken fingers and French fries."

"A part of me is looking forward to the day where you can no longer eat crap and still look this good, so you'll be forced to make a change."

"Let's hope I've got at least another decade of fast metabolism left."

"You're crazy," he says with a smile. "Okay, so this weekend... date number two...and a half. There's this Croatian festival on Saturday night I think would be a lot of fun. It'll have a bunch of food vendors and live music and stuff. Would you want to go?"

"For sure. That sounds fun."

"Yeah, and we don't have to stay there all night if it's lame. We can figure out something else to do afterward."

I wake up on Saturday full of energy and excitement. I get to see Mark tonight. Of course I can't risk my mom seeing him pick me up. Instead, I meet him at his house so he can drive us to the festival. I'm sure as heck not ready to meet his parents, so he comes outside after I park my car on the street.

We arrive at the festival to find a winding row of white tents leading to a stage with a band playing a song I've never heard before. We head straight for the tents selling food. I look up at one of them to find a menu incomprehensible to me.

I turn to Mark and say, "All right, you need to help me out here."

"All right, trust me with this. You'll like what I choose."

"Okay, make sure it has a lot of carbs and fat."

"Say no more. I've got you covered."

After Mark orders a few different things for us, we sit down at a small table nearby.

"All right, we'll start with a burek. Bread, meat, and cheese. Foolproof."

I bite into it and find that it's delicious. "Yum!"

"It's loaded with fat and carbs, just as you requested. I figured you'd like it. Next up is cevapcici. It's like a meatball, but more flavorful."

"Two for two, Mark," I say after tasting one.

"Okay, the last thing is a dessert, so let's save that until the end."

The dessert, called rozata, is delicious as well. It's like flan with a caramel topping.

"Look at you, expanding your horizons," Mark says.

"I know. I feel so cultured. So, have you ever been to Croatia?"

"Yeah, it's awesome. I still have some family there. What's your nationality?"

"Mostly Irish."

"That's what I thought. Have you ever been to Ireland?"

"No. I've been to Europe, though. My sister was studying abroad in France, so we visited her."

"You like it?"

"Yeah. I mean, I was only eleven so I didn't really appreciate it. This festival is cool, though. It's funny how things like this exist without my ever knowing it."

"I know. There are so many niche things like this, but unless it's your interest, you wouldn't know. I'm sure there are Irish festivals all year round."

"You're probably right. All right, I have a question," I say, switching topics. "Well, multiple questions."

"I'm ready."

"Amy…"

"Ah."

"I guess I'm just more curious and fascinated than anything. The last girl I dated was in sixth grade, and we never even kissed. Oh, and by the way, that girl was Kara." Mark laughs. "But you were in a long-term relationship recently. So what was it like? Was something missing?"

"Well, that was my only serious relationship. She's Croatian too, and her parents are friends with mine, so I've known her for a while. I wasn't in love with her, but I did have strong feelings. We were very comfortable together and had fun when we hung out."

"Okay, but I'm guessing you guys were physical. So..."

"So how was that?" he asks. I nod. "It was good. I mean, I was attracted to her. That's why all this is confusing to me. I had a genuine attraction toward her. But I'm much more attracted to you." I feel myself blush as a smile comes to my face. "Especially when you smile like that."

"Oh, stop," I say. "But what you said makes sense. It's not like you can only be attracted to guys or girls. There's a gray area."

"Yeah. Unfortunately, I don't think most people would agree with you."

I ask my last question regarding Amy. "So why did things end between you two? I know you said something just felt off."

"Yeah, it came to where I could take it or leave it. I still cared for her, but it felt like a friendship toward the end."

"Got it."

"Any more questions?"

"Nope."

"Satisfied?"

"Yes."

"Okay, now it's your turn to tell me about your relationship with Kara."

I laugh. "Oh boy. It was super intense. We would go to Friday Night Skate every week and hold hands. And then we would write each other notes and pass them during class."

"Wow. So how did it end?"

"I wrote a break-up letter and made Natalie give it to her at recess."

"Ouch. Harsh."

"That's not as bad as how I broke up with my fifth-grade girlfriend. When the bell rang on the last day of school, I had my friend walk up to her and tell her 'we're done.'"

Mark shakes his head. "Heartbreaker. So have you ever done anything physical with a girl?"

"No, just made out with a couple girls. Actually, not even. It was more like French kissing for a few seconds."

"Okay, another question," he says.

"Keep 'em coming."

"When did you first—or when did you officially know that you're gay?"

"Well, I've always known really, but I was too young to admit it. Like, I remember being attracted to guys in grade school. But it wasn't until early last year that I actually admitted it to myself. And building on what you said about your attraction to Amy, I think I might have had genuine attraction to some girls. In seventh grade I had my first kiss with a girl, and I remember wanting to do it. I don't know. I was thirteen, so it's hard to remember how I felt back then. Maybe it was just curiosity, not attraction." Mark nods. "I'm not being very articulate right now."

"No, I understand," he says. "It's hard to explain. I'm trying to compare your experience to mine. So if you were attracted to guys in grade school, why did it take you until junior year to admit it?"

"Honestly, because admitting it meant that I would need to tell my family at some point. I'm still terrified of telling them, but I don't think about it much because it's not going to happen in the near future. But something switched in my brain last year. I thought, 'Screw it. I'm attracted to guys. There's nothing I can do about it.' I realized I couldn't lie about it my whole life."

"So would your family really have an issue with it?"

"I know my mom would. Not sure about my sisters. It would probably be a mixed bag of reactions."

"So you don't have *any* attraction to girls?" Mark asks.

"No. I can tell when a girl is hot, but I don't have any sexual attraction toward them. Whereas my attraction to guys—wow. All right, my turn to ask. Am I the first guy you've ever been attracted to?"

After a pause, he hesitantly says, "No…but you're the first guy I've had feelings for."

"Darn right."

I can tell the wheels in Mark's head are spinning. Maybe his sexuality isn't as black and white as mine. After all, he did have a long-term girlfriend. But some gay guys marry women before coming to terms with their sexuality. That doesn't make them any less gay.

After finishing our dessert, we head to the stage to hear the band perform. They're not bad, but it's not my style of music. Mark senses correctly.

"You don't like them," he says.

"They're...they're fine."

He laughs. "I love that you can't say a mean thing about anyone."

"I try not to. The lead guy has a pretty good voice actually. But yeah, I wouldn't buy their album."

Fortunately, this band is on the tail end of their set. They are followed by a mellower guy and girl duo with an acoustic vibe. The girl has a great voice, and I honestly enjoy a couple of their songs. I can always appreciate a good singer.

The festival winds down at about ten, so Mark and I head out shortly after. After he pulls into his driveway, we both get out of the car in the dark, quiet night. I look up at his house, trying to see if anyone inside is watching us, knowing that the likelihood is low.

"Let me walk you to your car," Mark says.

"Needless to say, I had an awesome time tonight," I say as we walk down his driveway.

"Me too."

We stop at the driver's side of my car as I rest my back up against the door. I look back at his house again.

"No one is watching us," he says.

"Are you sure?" He nods.

He and I are inches away from each other. I want to kiss him. I have to kiss him.

"Get home safely," he says as he gives me a hug.

As we let go of our embrace, I move my hands from his back to his face as I go in for a kiss. I keep my lips touching his for a few seconds before releasing them and going in for another kiss. I pull back and exhale loudly. Wow. It takes me a moment to recover.

He smiles at me before grabbing my waist to pull me in for another kiss. After a few more seconds, he pulls back. "Mmm," he grunts.

"Your lips...are so soft," I say. "They're like two big pillows." He laughs. "Seriously. I need to do that one more time before I let you go. Come here." I give him another kiss.

"You're a really good kisser," he says.

"Well, thank God because it's been years since I've kissed anyone. You're really good too."

"All right, give me another hug."

And with a hug and one final, lingering kiss, I open my car door and drive away. How did I go so many years without letting myself experience this? Those kisses were so intense. It never felt like that when I kissed a girl. I'll be replaying this new experience with Mark in my mind all week.

CHAPTER TEN

It's Sunday, which means that I only have one more night to prepare for my *Anything Goes* audition. Fortunately, I have a lesson with my voice teacher, Linda, tonight. It's only a half hour a week, but I love going. Of course I love it—it's me singing nonstop show tunes to an audience of one.

Due to the holidays and finals, it's been a few weeks since my last lesson. For my audition song, she and I have decided on "Dames" from *42nd Street*. I'm sure I could find a better one, but the song fits the style of the show and is good for my range. Before diving into it, I sing a couple other songs to get warmed up.

After about ten minutes, Linda says to me, "Okay, something is different about you."

"What do you mean?"

"I don't know. You just seem so much more free and relaxed. And happy."

"Really?"

"Yes. What is going on?"

"Nothing. I mean, I'm definitely happy, but nothing's changed." Of course I have to lie.

"All right," she says. "Well, whatever it is, it's working for you. It's like the weight of the world was lifted off your shoulders or something."

I can't believe she senses a change. Mark's effect on me is stronger than I thought.

The next day, auditions start shortly after the final bell rings. It's always exciting and fun to watch everyone sing their hearts out for their desired roles. Some will sound amazing, some will sound awful, and most will sound average. Where will I fall?

Natalie decides to audition early on—the first time she's early for anything in her life. She likes to get it over with while I like to scope out the competition first. She does a beautiful rendition of "So In Love" from *Kiss Me, Kate*. That combined with her tap-dancing skills should secure her a callback for the lead.

About twenty minutes later, Chris auditions with "Tonight" from *West Side Story*. He joins Natalie and me in our seats as we watch a girl we don't know walk up to the stage. She sings a beautiful song that I've never heard before and nails it. The girl's voice is seriously amazing. Chris and I turn to Natalie to see her reaction.

"Crap," Natalie says, looking forward.

"Hopefully she can't dance?" I say to her.

"Hopefully seniority plays a factor?" Chris says. "She's got to be a freshman."

"Who was better—me or her?" Natalie asks.

Chris and I remain silent for a couple seconds, trying to think of what to say.

"Guys?" Natalie says.

"You both were great," I quickly say.

"And you're a better dancer," Chris says. "I'm sure of it."

Toward the end of the day, I finally audition. The tempo of the song was faster than I expected, but I still do pretty well. It's enough to earn me a callback for the next day. Natalie got one as well.

We show up for callbacks the next day to find only six people there, including us. That's it? No wonder Chris didn't get called back.

Sure enough, the freshman girl with the flawless voice is there. Fortunately for Natalie, she didn't do so great during the dance portion of yesterday's audition.

After doing various readings and songs from the show, we all head home. The process was much quicker than I expected.

"We've got this, right?" I say to Natalie as we leave.

"*You've* got it. I don't know about me."

"I think we both pulled it off."

The director calls us both that night to confirm our hopes.

I'm really liking this new year so far. I've gotten everything I wanted: Mark and I are off to a great start, I have the lead in the play, and I've got a great group of colleges to choose from.

❖

As I'm pouring my usual morning bowl of cereal a few days later, my mom walks into the kitchen for what seems like her usual interrogation.

"Where did you go last night?" I'm hoping this is part of her normal questioning, but her tone and look make me think she knows something.

"Just went to dinner and then back to Natalie's." Lie. I actually spent the night with Mark and told my friends I had a family thing.

"Who was there?"

"The usual crew."

"Who?" she asks without skipping a beat.

"Natalie, Kara, Chris, Reese." After rattling off four names, I fear that I should have kept it to two or three. I walk into the living room to get away from the conversation, but she follows me.

"So what do you and your friends do when you hang out?"

"Talk, laugh, watch TV…"

"I know what kids your age do," she says, acting like I'm trying to fool her.

"What, drink? You know I don't do that."

"I'm sure some of your friends are having sex."

Whoa, where did that come from? "Actually, no. We're all virgins." Okay, Kara isn't, but that's none of my mom's business.

"Oh, right. Chris is a virgin?"

"Yes. I'm being a hundred percent honest."

"Well, does he date guys?"

"Yeah, he has."

"Well, how does he know he's gay?"

Crap. "I guess he knows who he's attracted to and that's guys."

Then suddenly, she asks, "So, are you gay?"

My heart has been beating so fast it feels like it finally gave out. I'm speechless as I make a split-second decision. I could tell her now and never have to worry about it ever again, or I could lie and postpone this conversation until I'm prepared for it.

"Yeah," I respond, seemingly involuntarily. As soon as the word comes out of my mouth, the tears start to fall from her eyes.

"But I don't want you to be gay." As she is sitting across from me, I keep thinking that this isn't real. How is this happening right now? I can't come up with a response, so she continues. "So have you acted on this?"

"Yeah," I say with no hesitation. What the hell am I doing? "Just kissing," I quickly add. Hey, it's the truth.

"No. This needs to stop."

"Okay." Dear God, get me out of this conversation.

"I mean, don't you think that this is wrong?"

"No. I can't control who I'm attracted to."

"I think you're confused."

"Okay."

"So your friends know?"

"My close friends, yeah."

"Okay, well, you're not telling any of your sisters."

As if I could handle this conversation with any of them. "Okay. I'm going to the gym." The only way to get out of this situation is to physically remove myself.

"Don't be telling your friends about this talk," she adds as I head upstairs to change.

As soon as I get into my car, my phone is to my ear, ringing Natalie.

"Hola," she answers.

"Natalie," I say in a serious tone.

"What's wrong?"

"I was just talking to my mom…"

"Oh no. She knows?"

"She does now."

"Oh gosh, I'm sorry. Where are you now?"

"Driving nowhere."

"Come to my house."

"Okay."

Knowing I'll probably have to see Natalie's parents, I pull myself together and prepare to put on a smile. Before I can get to the door, Natalie opens it.

"Hey," I say.

"What do you need? Junk food? Water?"

"No, I'm fine. Thanks." She and I slip into her basement. I'm not sure where her parents are, but I'm glad I don't have to make small talk with them.

"Okay, what happened?" she asks.

"First she starts asking me about my night and where I went." Oh, no. I realize that as far as Natalie knows, I was with family last night. I quickly move the story along so she doesn't have time to interrupt. After a few minutes, my recap is done.

"Gosh, I'm sorry," she says. "I think this was just her immediate reaction and it will get better with time. She's in shock now."

"Yeah, I hear you. It's still going to be so awkward at home."

"So wait, what *did* you do last night? I thought you stayed in."

"Um…" I try to think of a lie but can't come up with one that Natalie would actually believe.

"Brendan? You lied to me?"

"Crap. Yes. I went out with someone, but I can't tell you who it was."

"What? A date?"

"You could say that."

"Do I know him?"

My hesitation answers the question.

"Who is it?" she asks.

"Natalie, I can't say. Seriously, I would never betray his trust. He isn't out to anyone, and I can't be responsible for telling people."

"So was this a first date, or have you been seeing him a while?"

"Just a first date. And it's probably going to be the last. It was kind of dull."

"You're killing me here."

"I know. It's really not that juicy, though. You wouldn't care much." Another lie to try to get her to lay off the subject. I can't risk her investigating in case I give away too much.

Natalie and I chat for another half hour or so before I tell her I should get back home. She's made me feel a lot better, but the one person I really want to see right now is Mark.

While Natalie and I were talking, I was slyly texting him to see if he could meet me somewhere to talk. I'm not ready to face my mom yet, and I can't risk talking to him on the phone at home.

After leaving Natalie's, I head straight to Starbucks to meet him. I already texted him that my mom found out, so when I arrive at the coffee shop, he is standing inside, ready to comfort me.

"Hi," I say after opening the door. "Hug me."

We are always discreet in public because God knows if we'll run into someone we know, but today I don't care. He gives me a tight hug and rubs my back with his hands.

"Are you okay?" he asks.

"Yes. I'll tell you about it when we sit down."

After getting our drinks and finding a table in the back, naturally, I recap the conversation between my mom and me.

"So I don't get it. What prompted her to ask?" he says.

"Good question. I think it's a combination of reasons. One, she's realizing that I've gone through four years of high school without showing an ounce of interest in a girl. Plus most of my friends are girls or gay guys. Also, she knows that Chris and I are close and that he's out. She's finally facing what's been in front of her my whole life."

"Man, I'm sorry. Do you think she's on to us?"

"No, I think this conversation would have happened today regardless of our situation. It's just bad timing. I didn't want to have to deal with this yet."

"I know. Did she ask if you're dating anyone?"

I smile. "You're worried, aren't you?"

"No, no, I'm just wondering if she dug any further...okay, yes, I'm slightly worried."

"No, she didn't ask me that, but she did ask if I ever acted on my attractions and I said yes because I'm an idiot."

He laughs. "Brendan. See, you're not used to lying to your mom, so you suck at it."

"Exactly."

"Do you think she's going to be super strict now? Especially since she probably thinks you're 'acting on it' all around town."

"I don't know. I'll need to make sure my alibis are airtight if I'm hanging out with you alone...which brings me to a question I have for you."

"You're putting on your charming smile. That means you want something from me."

"Correct. Okay, obviously my friends don't know about us. However, it would be so much easier if I could let Kara in on the secret. First off, I might go insane if I keep it in any longer. Partly because I like you a lot, and I want to share that with her. But also, I really think I'll need to vent to someone other than you when it comes to my mom and hiding our relationship from her and all that. I don't want to put that all on you."

He's about to say something, but I cut him off. "Also—and this is the main reason I want to tell her—it will be so much easier to lie to my mom if I know Kara will cover for me. Kara will always be a reliable alibi.

"So for example," I continue, "if I see a movie with you but tell my mom I went with Kara, I can tell Kara, 'By the way, I told my mom that you and I are seeing a movie together tonight if she happens to call you or something.'"

He nods, understanding. "I hear you."

"And I know what you're thinking. Are we sure Kara can keep this a secret? The girl is a lockbox. I could tell her *anything*, and she wouldn't betray my trust. I think it's partly because she doesn't care enough to tell other people."

"Are you *sure*? Because, Brendan, if it gets back to Chris or someone else at school…"

"I know. It would suck. I promise you one million percent that she wouldn't tell anyone. There's a bigger risk in having someone see us here right now."

"Speaking of, I thought the girl sitting behind you is my neighbor, but I think I'm wrong." He leans to his right to take a peek over my shoulder. I laugh.

"Okay, back to this," he says. "You trust Kara…I trust you…so yes, you can tell her."

"Thank you," I sigh.

"Wait a minute, has she known this whole time but you just didn't tell me?"

"No, I swear. So how should I tell her? Send her a picture of us kissing?"

He stares at me, not amused. "Then instead of sending it to Kara, you accidently send it to your sister or something."

"Eek. Well, on a serious note, Mark, today has been rough and talking with you has been really nice. You helped me laugh in a tough situation."

"I'm sorry you have to deal with this. Give me an update tonight on how the rest of the day goes with your mom," he says, placing his hands on my legs underneath the table.

"I will. It's tough because it's just her and me at home, you know? No one's around to buffer the situation." He looks on with his adorable face and glowing eyes. "I really want to kiss you right now," I say, not expecting him to go with it. "Just a quick one."

He looks over my shoulder again at the girl who may or may not be his neighbor. "All right, let's do it," he says, apparently convinced it's not her.

My eyes widen. "Really?"

"You've had a rough day."

I smile and lean in to kiss him. After a few seconds, I pull back.

"One more," he whispers, his eyes still closed.

I laugh and lean in again to give one more kiss. After chatting for a little while longer, Mark and I say good-bye, and I head back to reality. On my way home, I call Kara. Mark has a soccer game tonight, so I think it's a perfect time to tell Kara about him and me.

"Hello?" I hear from the other end of the line.

"Brace yourself, Kara."

"What?"

"Are you free tonight? Because I have a couple things to tell you."

"I'm free. Is this bigger than your coming out to me?"

"Um…"

"Come on."

"Okay, maybe not quite. Well, first off, I won't go into details now, but my mom asked me if I'm gay today and I said yes."

"What?"

"Yeah, so I'll tell you about that, but then I have other news as well, which is more fun."

"And I have to wait until tonight to find out? Why do you love surprises so much?"

I laugh. "I don't know. Can we just hang at your place?"

"Sure. I'm going to work out and shower. Does seven work?"

"Perfect. See you then."

I come home to find an empty house. Thank God. I'm still not ready to face my mom, although I know I'll never be ready. I'm hoping to leave before she gets back.

After showering, I make some pasta for dinner. While I'm cooking, the door leading from the garage to the kitchen opens and my mom walks in with groceries.

Neither of us says hi. "Can you put these away?" I stop stirring my pasta to put the groceries away. After another minute of silence, she chimes in with, "What are you doing tonight?"

"Going to Kara's."

"Okay, well listen, I don't want you talking to your friends about our conversation today." Apparently she doesn't remember she already told me that.

"Okay."

"Who's going over there?"

"Just me."

She walks away. Cooking and eating occupies the next twenty minutes of my time. Fortunately, after that, it's almost time to head out.

I arrive at Kara's a few minutes early. She greets me in sweats and a T-shirt.

"Aw, you dressed up for me," I say.

"I know. You like it?"

We walk into her living room so I can greet her parents. They've always been so nice to me. Even though Kara hasn't said anything to them, I think they know I'm not a threat to their daughter.

"Well, look who it is," her dad says.

"Hi, Brendan," her mom follows.

"Hello, how are you guys?"

"We're good," Kara's mom says. "So Kara tells us that you still haven't decided on a school for next year."

"No. I'm waiting until the last minute. I have trouble committing, apparently."

"Well, that's all right," Kara's dad says. "Kara is the same way. We're still waiting for her to decide."

Kara is debating whether to go to Northwestern or Cornell. She and I have always competed when it comes to academics. A part of me feels like I need to go to an equally prestigious school so that she doesn't show me up.

I would never tell her this, but I actually think she's smarter than I am…barely. She beat me on the SAT, but I'm superior when it comes to the ACT. It's cool because we have opposite strengths. If we combined my math score with her verbal score, we'd be brilliant.

"I'm hoping she goes with Northwestern," I say. "I'm much more likely to visit Chicago with my sisters there."

"All right, we're going to go downstairs," Kara says to her parents, eager to end the conversation.

"All right," her mom says. "Well, Kara, offer Brendan something to eat."

"I will, I will. He knows where the food is."

I grab some Cool Ranch Doritos from the cupboard and a bottle of water from the fridge and head downstairs with Kara. After sitting down on the couch in her basement and turning on the TV for background noise, we get to business.

"Okay," I say.

"I'm ready."

"Let's get the bad story out of the way. My mom." This is the third time I'm telling the story today, and I really don't feel like going into the details again, so I recap as quickly as possible.

Kara offers her always supportive and logical advice. "Okay, your mom is probably in disbelief and doesn't want it to be true, so right now she will say anything to try to snap you out of it. But as time goes on, she'll realize it's not something that's going to change." I nod. That's basically what Natalie said too. "I think the good news is that it's out of the way. You don't have to worry about it anymore."

"That's true. All right, I've thought about this way too much today. Let's move on to the fun news." I've been waiting to tell someone this and am so excited to finally spill my guts out to her.

"Okay wait, before you say anything, please tell me that I'm not the first person you're telling this." I smile at her. "Brendan. Our friends are going to hate me."

"I know, I know. But Kara, this news...I won't be telling anyone else. I *want* to, trust me. The only reason I can tell you is because I got permission from the person that this thing involves."

She scrunches her forehead, trying to figure out what it is that I'm about to tell her. "Okay, I have no idea where this is going. Shoot."

"Okay. I'm trying to decide whether I should ease into this news or just dramatically say what it is and then explain how I got there."

"The latter. Duh."

I laugh. "Okay, ready? I'm dating Mark Galovic."

Her jaw drops and is frozen for a few seconds. "Oh…my gosh."

I sit in front of her smiling. "Wait, how long have—?"

"Like two weeks. Since the night of the basketball game, actually."

"Really? You guys are good; I had no idea."

"That's good to hear. I've been acting my butt off when I'm with him in front of other people."

"Okay, I still need an explanation. How did this happen? Apparently he did a one-eighty from New Year's?"

I tell Kara the details of Mark's reveal to me and how we've managed to keep it a secret thus far.

"Wow," she says. "So many questions. First, none of his friends know that he's even gay, right?"

"Right. And he's actually never said that he's gay. I think he felt pressure to define his sexuality because of the feelings he has for me, but I told him not to worry about it, so I think he's shelved that for a while."

"I can understand that. For you, it was easy to accept that you're gay, right? Like, it wasn't this long internal struggle."

"Yeah, I mean, I suppressed it all the time growing up, but once I let all of that suppression go last year, it was easy for me to say, 'Okay, I'm gay.' There was no 'Maybe I'm bi or maybe this is a one-time attraction to a guy.' "

"Okay, next question. Have you been able to hang out with him one-on-one a lot? What do you tell your mom?"

"A pretty good amount so far. Either after school or on the weekends…like last night when I lied to you."

"You jerk."

"And then I tell my mom that I'm hanging with you or Natalie or whomever. But now that she knows I'm gay, it's going to be a lot harder, which is where you come in."

"Oh gosh. I'm your go-to alibi now, aren't I?"

"Pretty much. The bottom line is if my mom gets crazy enough to call you or your parents and asks if we were together on such and such night, say yes."

"Great."

"I doubt it will ever come to that. I don't know how this is going to play out."

"I'm sure it'll be fine, but if I were you, I'd think about what you'd say if you get caught. Do you admit it? Do you say Mark is a friend?"

"You're right. I'll think about all the scenarios that could play out. It's like an improv class. Fun."

"Totally. Okay, next question. How's it going? Do you really like him? Is it what you expected?"

"It's amazing. He's so nice, and funny, and cute. I could go on and on."

"Okay, let's get juicier. Have you guys done anything physical?"

I laugh. "It's been two weeks."

"I know, I know."

"Just kissing, which is amazing, by the way. You've seen his lips. They're as soft as they look. But we're taking things slowly since it's the first experience for both of us."

"Yeah, I figured. But even if you wanted to go further, where would you do it? I mean, you never hang out at each other's places, right? It's always out in public."

"It's funny that you say that because Mark actually just mentioned hanging out at his place next week for the first time. He doesn't think his parents would suspect anything."

"Oh boy, meeting the parents," Kara says.

"I know. But they'll think I'm a friend so I won't feel the pressure to impress...I hope?"

"Well, I think that would be nice. It would probably get old hanging out in public where you can't show affection toward each other."

"Yeah. Even just watching a movie on the couch at his place would be so nice. And he said he and his friends always hang out in the basement so if he and *I* did that, his parents wouldn't think twice about it."

"Perfect. Then you can get privacy without worrying."

❖

The next week at home is tense, to say the least. My mom and I keep our talking to a minimum, and when we do speak, our words have a hint of passive aggressiveness. Fortunately, she doesn't bring up the gay thing at all. I'm not sure what else there is to say at this point. She made her feelings crystal clear the other day. This whole situation would be so much easier if it weren't just her and me at home. If only one of my sisters still lived here, she'd be able to buffer the situation without even realizing it.

Being the youngest sibling in a family is great in many ways. I was spoiled and babied when I was younger, constantly getting attention. I was also a bit overprotected, but in a caring way. My sisters tell me how my dad used to always call home from work to ask how I was doing. They joke that he didn't care about them—just about his baby boy. I felt a constant wave of love.

But as I got older, I noticed that the attention was still on me, but in a somewhat overbearing way. I'm sure my sisters look at me as a naïve seventeen-year-old who needs guidance and advice even when I don't ask for it. They will always be older than I am. Therefore, they will probably always think they know better than I do.

For a little while, I was considering majoring in musical theater at college. Performing Arts is my strongest passion, so naturally I was considering whether I could make a career out of it. Ultimately, I determined that it wasn't the right path for me, but instead of letting me figure that out myself, my sister, Phoebe, told me I was making a mistake. Her approach wasn't delicate, either. It was blunt and direct, making it seem like I was stupid for ever thinking that theater would be a good choice.

Maybe I'm being oversensitive. I wish my feelings and thoughts weren't automatically dismissed because of my age. I would have appreciated her input if she had said, "Have you thought about this?" or "What if this happens?"

I'm not saying that being the youngest is the hardest. Being the oldest actually seems even worse. I think about how my sister, Sarah, had to step up when my dad died. She had to help my mom plan the wake, the funeral, and God knows what else. Luckily, I was shielded from all that. Plus the oldest one seems to have the strictest rules because the parents are paranoid. As the youngest, I've had barely any rules. Unfortunately, I get the sense that that might change now that my mom knows I'm gay.

CHAPTER ELEVEN

"They're going to love you," Mark says to me as I try to pick an outfit for the night. "And remember, they don't know we're dating, so don't feel pressure to impress them. To them, you're just another friend."

"I know."

"All right, but you still sound nervous."

"I'm *so* nervous. I'm not worried about them liking me. You know parents love me."

"He says modestly."

I laugh. "I'm worried that they're going to suspect something is going on with us."

"How?" he asks.

"I don't know. They could get the sense that I'm gay and then realize that you and I have hung out a lot recently, and then put two and two together."

"No. My parents don't think that way, you'll see. They know Chris and I are friends but have never once asked me about our friendship."

"That's true."

"Just be yourself. Besides, I'll introduce you to them, we'll have a casual dinner, and then we can go downstairs and have privacy."

"Okay," I say, feeling slightly better. "And would they come down to check up on us?"

"No, they'll leave us alone. I have friends over all the time. I've never betrayed their trust, so they've always given me my space."

"Okay."

"Pick an outfit yet?" he asks. I can imagine his teasing smile as he says it.

"Nope."

"Wear something tight to show off your arms."

"How about a tank top?"

"Even better."

"All right, I'm going to shower and get ready. Seven o'clock?"

"Yes!"

"Okay, see you soon!"

Seconds after I hang up my phone, I hear a knock on my door. Crap. "Yeah?" I say.

My mom opens the door. "Who were you talking to?" How long has she been standing there? What did she hear? She was downstairs when I started talking to Mark but somehow walked upstairs without my noticing.

Instead of lying, I decide to push back a little. "Why do you always ask me that?"

"Because I want to know who my seventeen-year-old son is talking to."

"I was talking to Kara. We're hanging out tonight just like we do every weekend. You know I don't drink, you know I don't smoke, you know I don't do drugs, *and* I've told you multiple times that I'm a virgin. What else do you want from me?"

"I want to make sure you're not hanging out with some guy, because if you are, it has to stop. Enough is enough."

"Nope, no guy. I guess you want me to be single for the rest of my life, right? Or maybe I should marry a girl?"

"I want you to get past this phase and snap back into reality," she says.

It's my fault for opening up this can of worms right now, but I refuse to let her ruin my night. I decide to end the conversation.

"I have to shower," I say.

Fortunately, it works. She leaves my doorway and heads to her bedroom. I finally settle on an outfit when I hear my sister, Maggie, call my name from downstairs.

"Yeah?" I yell back.

"Can you come here for a minute?"

I bolt downstairs to find her sitting in front of the computer.

"Come here."

"What?" I say, realizing she wants to show me something on the computer.

"I just pulled up 'Recent Files,'" she says quietly, "and this is what's in there."

I bend down to get a closer look at the name of the files. The first two are Word documents: "AP French Lit Essay 6" and "Research Paper Draft v3."

The next three are picture files. My face turns white as I read the graphic sexual descriptions. I am frozen in shock. How did this happen? How am I so stupid as to forget to delete these files forever? I'm losing it. I don't move until Maggie says something.

"I don't care, but you probably want to delete these before Mom sees."

"Okay," I say, nodding. I'm so mortified that I can't stand there for another second. I head upstairs and immediately go into the shower. *Please let Maggie be gone when I get out*, I think. I don't want to face her again, at least not today.

After showering, I get ready for my night with Mark. I figure as long as I stay upstairs in my room, I'm safe.

It takes about twenty minutes, but finally my state of denial ends, and I'm able to accept what just happened. Now it's time for me to look at the bright side. First, my mom did not find these. If she had, it would have been *awful*. Second, Maggie seemed unfazed by it. Clearly she's not shocked to know that I'm into guys. That's one less person to whom I have to worry about coming out.

By the time I'm ready to leave, I'm able to put the last hour behind me. My focus returns to my night with Mark and my introduction to his parents, as if that makes me feel less stressed.

I park my car on the street directly outside of his house and take a deep breath before getting out. With each step toward his front door, my heart rate increases. I finally make it to the door and knock three times. Please let Mark answer and not his parents.

The door opens to reveal Mark smiling. "Hey, Brendan, what's up?"

"Hey, not much," I say. I start to go in for a hug but then remember where I am. Whoops. *We're just friends tonight*, I remind myself as my arms come back down to my side.

He laughs before whispering, "You're nervous." Then in full voice he says, "Come on in."

I walk behind him through the foyer into the kitchen to find his mom at the stove with her back to us. She has the same blond hair as Mark and is also almost as tall as he is.

"Mom, this is Brendan," Mark says to her. She turns around to look at me.

"Brendan, hi. How are you?" she says before shaking my hand.

"Hi, I'm good. Nice to meet you," I say with a big smile.

"You too. Now you're friends with Chris, right?"

"Yeah, I've known him since grade school."

"Oh, wow. And then you do theater with him too?"

"Right," I say, noticing that the kitchen opens up into a large living room. I do a quick scan of the area but can't see Mark's dad anywhere. I pray he's as nice as Mark's mom.

"Are you guys hungry yet?" Mrs. Galovic says. "I'm making pasta."

"Yeah, that sounds great," I say. Thank God she's cooking something I like. Based on my palate, the odds were not in her favor.

"When will it be ready?" Mark asks his mom.

"We're waiting for your dad and sister to come home, but it shouldn't be too much longer."

"Okay, we're going to go downstairs," Mark says. "Let us know when it's done."

I wait until we're all the way down the basement stairs before I let out a huge sigh of relief.

He laughs. "Are you good? Harmless, right?" I nod. "Oblivious, right?"

"Yes."

"All right, now come here," he says as he pulls me into his arms and gives me a kiss. We keep kissing as we move to the couch.

"Now I have to impress them through a whole dinner," I say between kisses.

"Piece of cake. And we'll eat fast so we can get back to this."

About five minutes later, we hear the basement door open, which scares the crap out of me as I scoot away from Mark.

"Mark?" his mom says.

"Yeah?"

"Dinner's ready. You want to come up?"

"Okay."

I stand up but realize my make-out session with Mark has caused quite the bulge in my pants. "Crap, hold on," I say. "Let me readjust."

I notice that he's in the same predicament.

"Okay, think of something non-sexual," he says, laughing.

"Dead puppies, dead puppies."

"What?"

"That's what they teach you in theater if you have to be serious in a scene but can't stop laughing," I explain.

"Okay, you go with that while I think of history class."

I close my eyes for a few seconds. "All right, I'm good," I say after looking down at myself. "Well, good enough."

"Okay, walk slowly. I need a few more seconds."

I lead the way as we creep up the stairs. Once we get to the top, I make Mark go ahead of me. We get to the kitchen and find Mark's dad and sister sitting at the table while Mrs. Galovic is near the stove again.

"Dad, Eva, this is Brendan," Mark says.

"Hey, Brendan," Eva says. She knows me, but we've never officially met.

Mark's dad looks at me. "Brendan, nice to meet you," he says, reaching out his hand.

"Thanks, you too."

"Sit down, guys," Mark's mom says. "I'll bring everything over."

I take a seat to the right of Eva, diagonally across from Mr. Galovic, who is reading the newspaper, while Mark sits to the right of me at the head of the table.

"Brendan, are you doing *Anything Goes*?" Eva asks.

"Yeah, we started rehearsals this week."

"What part did you get?"

"Billy."

"Nice!"

"Is that a big part?" Mrs. Galovic asks.

"It's the lead, right?" Eva says to me.

"Yep."

"That's great," Mrs. Galovic says as she brings the last dish of food to the table.

"Why didn't you audition?" I ask Eva. Talking to her calms my nerves while I try to get a read on Mark's dad, who continues to look down at his paper.

"I couldn't. I do soccer in the spring."

Mark's mom sits across from me next to Mr. Galovic, which prompts him to fold up the newspaper and toss it on the counter behind him.

"Looks great," he says, eyeing the food.

"Mark, start," Mrs. Galovic says, handing the bowl of pasta to him.

After a few minutes of family chitchat, during which I sit quietly and observe, the questioning turns to me.

"So, Brendan," Mark's dad says, "do you go to Saint Xavier?"

"Yep."

"You don't play soccer, do you?"

"No," I say, not knowing what else to add.

"He plays tennis," Mark says. "He got third in state last year."

"Wow, good for you," Mr. Galovic says. "I played tennis when I was younger. Wasn't too good, but I enjoyed it. It's a great sport."

I'm happy when Eva interrupts her dad's line of questioning. "What are you guys doing tonight?"

"Just watching a movie here," Mark answers.

"You doing anything tonight?" I ask her. I'm taking any chance I can get to talk to her. It gives me a break from potential questioning from Mark's dad, although his questions so far have been harmless. I guess I'm worried that he's going to pick up on the fact that I'm gay.

"Yeah, I'm just hanging out at a friend's house," Eva answers.

"Which friend?" Mr. Galovic asks.

"Maura."

"Are any boys going to be there?"

"Oh my gosh, Dad," she replies. He continues to stare at her until she answers. "Yes."

"What are you going to be doing?"

His persistent questioning is exactly what I was afraid of. I'm glad I'm not on the receiving end.

"We're just going to be hanging out and talking," Eva answers.

"And there will be no alcohol there," Mark's dad says. The way he says it makes it seem more like an order as opposed to a question.

"No. And if there were, I wouldn't drink any," she adds with a condescending smile.

"Good answer," he says, finally satisfied.

"You know, you never grill Mark like this," Eva says.

"Well, with him, I don't have to worry about the threat of teenage boys." It takes everything in me not to sneak a peek at Mark.

"And you're right, I should grill Mark more," he continues. "Mark, will you be drinking tonight?"

"No, Dad," Mark says.

Mr. Galovic looks at me. "And, Brendan, will you be drinking?"

"No," I quickly say.

"Great. Satisfied?" he says, looking at Eva.

"You're not funny, Dad."

"You can't win with teenage girls," he says to me.

I give a smile and slight laugh. "I have five older sisters. I'm used to it."

"Five? You must be very patient," Mrs. Galovic says. "Your wife is going to be lucky."

This time I manage to give a slight smile to Mark. I spend the next ten minutes or so mostly observing Mark and his family. It's easy to see how much they care for each other.

After dinner, Mark and I head back downstairs.

"How harmless was that?" he asks.

"Thank God. I can relax now."

"You did great. I can tell my dad likes you."

"Yeah? Good."

"Should we pop in the movie?"

"Sure. So do you want to hear a funny story?" I ask Mark while he's getting the movie set up. "And by 'funny,' I mean 'mortifying.'"

"Go for it."

"Today, my sister, Maggie, found some porn of mine on our house computer."

His jaw drops. "*Gay* porn?"

I laugh. "Of course. Is there any other kind?"

"Oh my gosh," he says before laughing. "I'm sorry; I shouldn't laugh. So what did she say? Did she freak out?"

"No, not at all. Fortunately, she didn't care. She just told me to delete it before my mom sees it."

"Did she ask if you're gay or anything?"

"I think she got the answer to that question already."

"So did she, like, open up pictures or videos that you saved or what?"

"No…actually I don't know. I hope not! She just showed me some of the names of the files that were in the computer's 'Recent Files' list."

"Oh no," he says, starting to laugh again. "What were the names?"

"I blocked them from my memory. Probably 'hot Croatian guys' or something."

"Uh-huh. Trying to flatter me?"

"What do *you* like?"

He leans in. "I like kind…" He kisses me. "Smart…" Another kiss. "Adorable guys." I roll my eyes at him.

"You are so handsome," he says.

"Stop. No, I'm not."

"Come on. You know you are."

"I'll be honest with you," I say. "I think I have a good smile and I clean up nicely, but I'd be happy to change some things about my appearance."

"Like what?"

"I wish I weren't so pale. I wish my lips were big like yours. Oh, and my nose is crooked."

Mark laughs. "No, it's not. Let me see." I hold my head still so he can see my face straight on. "Okay, I *kind* of see it, but I would have never noticed that. Now it's *my* turn to be honest with you. Your smile *kills* me. It's one thing to be modest, but I want you to know how handsome you are."

"I will accept your compliment. I don't want you to think I'm super hard on myself. I have good self-esteem."

"Okay, good. Just making sure. I have things I want to change about myself too, you know."

"Can't wait to hear this," I say. "What?"

"My ass."

My jaw drops. "Are you kidding me? What about it?"

"It's too big."

"Oh my gosh. You're crazy! You have the best butt I've ever seen in my life."

"I love that you never say swear words. It cracks me up."

"Oh, because I said 'butt' instead of…"

"Ass. Yes."

"I swear occasionally. It makes more of a statement when I do it because people don't expect it."

"So when do you do it? When you're mad?"

"I guess so."

"But you never get mad."

"Which is why you've never heard me swear," I say with a smile.

"Hopefully I never will."

CHAPTER TWELVE

A s the school day is winding down the following Thursday, I get a text from Mark, asking me to call him as soon as my last class is done. I'm planning to pick up food with Chris before rehearsal starts, which leaves me about five minutes to talk on the phone in private. As soon as the bell rings, my phone is to my ear.

"Hey," Mark answers, sounding kind of serious.

"What's up?"

"Has Chris texted you?"

"No."

"Okay, good. I was in class with him today, and he was looking at something on my phone when you texted me. And my phone was on vibrate so I wasn't even paying attention."

"What did I say? It couldn't have been anything bad." I try to remember the texts I sent him today.

"No, it's not like you called me a pet name or something. It said, 'Have you looked into what movie we should see tomorrow?'"

Mark and I picked Friday to be our date night this coming weekend. Kelly has plans that night, so that's one less person to whom we have to lie.

"Crap," I say. "So he read it?"

"Yeah, he saw the text come through so he's like, 'Brendan texted you.' He started to read it out loud, and then his voice trailed off and he was like, 'You and Brendan are hanging out tomorrow?' He wasn't sure what to make of it."

"What'd you say?" I ask, praying he didn't say anything to dig the hole deeper.

"I said, 'Yeah, Brendan said he was going to ask everyone else if they wanted to go too. He didn't ask you yet?'"

"Perfect. Did that satisfy him?"

"I think so, but you need to invite him and everyone else ASAP."

"Aw, really? Can't we just say we're not going anymore or something? I don't want anyone else to come."

"I know, but it's just safer if we invite him. I don't want him to be any more suspicious than he already is."

"All right, fine. Maybe he can't even go anyway."

A few minutes later, I get to my car, where Chris is already standing. While we drive to get food, I decide to wait a little while to bring up the movie so as not to appear too obvious.

"Oh!" I say. "I was talking to Mark about seeing a movie this weekend. Any interest?"

"I was waiting for my invite."

"What do you mean?" Clearly I'm going to play dumb.

"I saw your text to Mark about it earlier."

"Oh, I was going to make my rounds. I swear."

"Who's going so far?"

"Well, Kelly can't hang out tomorrow, and I still need to ask Reese and Natalie…and Kara."

"Okay, so just you and Mark so far."

"Yeah, but we won't go if no one else can."

"Well, I can go. I'm working Saturday night, but I'm off tomorrow."

Great. Date night is ruined. I might as well invite everyone else now. At least I'll still be able to see Mark. More importantly, I think I'm successful at squashing Chris's suspicions.

After picking up food, Chris and I find a closer parking spot and head to rehearsal. Today we are learning a big dance number, which involves almost everyone in the cast. It will for sure be chaotic, but also a blast. About an hour into it, I ask Natalie about her weekend plans.

"None yet," she replies.

"Okay, well, Chris, Mark, and I were talking about maybe seeing a movie tomorrow night. You interested?"

"Just the four of us?"

"For now, yeah."

"I guess so," she says after debating for a few seconds.

Suddenly the doors of the auditorium swing open as our choreographer, Ned, makes his dramatic entrance. A tall black man with a feminine voice and a strut like a diva, we all assumed that he's gay. Apparently he has a girlfriend, but I'd like to see proof.

"All right, everyone, gather around," he yells.

The twenty or so of us group together as he explains what we will be doing today. He is teaching us the dance for the title song of the show, "Anything Goes." He tells us it involves multiple dance breaks, so we can't waste any time.

He wasn't kidding. As the closing song of the first act, it's a huge tap-dance number. I actually took a tap class with Natalie last summer so I'm pretty good, but my triple-time steps could definitely use some work. As the leads, she and I are placed front and center.

Tap's cool because you can fake the stuff that you can't do that well. The audience can't see whether someone is really getting in all the sounds that he's supposed to.

After three hours, the dance looks amazing—well, at least it feels amazing doing it. I'm not sure what it looks like to Ned.

"Not good enough!" he yells at us as we hold our final pose of the dance.

"Can we get a water break?" a girl yells.

"Give me one more run-through. If it's perfect, you can go home."

"If not?" Chris asks.

"It will be," Ned says, trying to encourage us after telling us we're not good enough.

Fortunately, he was right. After we run the dance again, a few of us collapse to the floor in exhaustion as Ned yells, "Yes! Yes! Thank you!"

❖

As planned, the next night, Chris, Natalie, Mark, and I go see a movie. Kara and Reese are busy tonight, although Kara told me that she would have loved to watch Mark and me try to behave like we're only friends.

Mark and I are the first ones to arrive at the theater.

"Maybe they won't show up?" I say to him as we stand side by side, looking out at the parking lot.

"Maybe we should ditch them before they do," he responds before giving me a nudge with his hip.

"Maybe there won't be four seats together in the theater, and we'll have to sit two and two!"

"Maybe the movie will be sold out," he says. "And we'll… um…I don't know where I was going with that one."

We both laugh. A few minutes later, all of our possible scenarios are dashed as our friends arrive and we successfully find four seats together in the theater. I don't even manage to sit next to Mark.

After the movie, we head to an ice cream shop to talk and hang out.

"Oh my gosh," Chris says right after we sit down. "I can't believe I forgot to tell you guys this."

"What?" Natalie and I say in unison.

"Guess who just came out?"

Nothing like a bit of gossip to perk me up. We all look at each other but can't think of any good guesses.

"Jeff Dietrich," Chris says.

"Wow, really?" I ask. I met Jeff last year during our school's musical. I'm not surprised that he's gay, but I guess I'm surprised he came out.

"Did Jeff tell you himself?" Mark asks Chris.

"No, he told Dave Nelson, who told me."

"Wait," Natalie says. "Isn't Jeff's dad…"

"A Theology teacher at our school," I say.

"Has Jeff told his dad yet?" Mark asks.

"God, no," Chris says.

"Well, he might be finding out soon," Natalie says.

"I don't know," I say. "I'd hope people wouldn't say anything to him."

"They better not," Mark says, probably more intensely than he planned. "It's not their place at all."

"Is that comment directed toward me?" Chris asks.

"No, I know you would never tell his dad or anything, but, yeah, I guess it's not your place to tell *us* even."

"Who are you guys going to tell?" Chris says.

"No one, but what if Jeff only wanted a few people to know and now the number is growing exponentially?"

"Honestly, I don't think he cares who knows," Chris says. "He's told a good number of people. I think he's ready to be out to everyone except his family. And I can keep a secret. I know some other people who are gay, and I haven't said a word because they aren't ready for people to know." He gives a subtle look toward me.

As the rest of the night progresses, so does my frustration that I have to treat Mark like a friend. It's been so long since we've hung out in a group, I forgot what it's like. It brings me back to the days when no one knew I was gay and I had to watch my every move around him.

A few minutes after getting into my car to head home for the night, my phone rings.

"Hi, Mark," I say.

"What's the matter?"

"Nothing," I say with an exhale.

"No? You were pretty quiet tonight."

"No."

"Yes, sir. Something was bothering you. I'm guessing I know what it is."

"What?"

"I think it was hard for you to have to treat me like a friend tonight. It was hard for *me*."

"It was. I just wanted to kiss you tonight."

"You sound so sad."

"No, I'm fine," I say, trying to not sound so dejected. "I promise. Tonight was just...I don't know. Harder than I thought it would be."

"Well, I wanted to kiss you too, so let's do it."

"I'm about to turn into my development."

"Look in your rearview mirror."

Mark is smiling and waving in the car behind me. After turning into my neighborhood, I pull over and turn my car off. I'm about to step out but he runs to my passenger side, opens the door, and sits down.

"There's that smile I was looking for tonight," he says.

I manage to stop smiling long enough to give him a kiss. "You're so cute," I say.

"It's the least I could do. I'm the reason we had to put on a charade tonight."

"It's okay. Like you said on our first date, it's best if we limit the number of group outings we have together. This is why. I mean, don't get me wrong. I still had fun."

"I understand," he says. "And I will no longer let Chris play with my phone in class."

"Speaking of Chris, you were getting pretty passionate talking about Jeff with him tonight."

"The kid's dad works at our school. What if it gets back to him?"

"I know, but Chris would never cross that line."

"But the more people that Chris tells, the greater the chance that Jeff's dad will find out."

"Good point. But look at me, for example. I'm confident that my friends haven't told anyone that I'm gay because I specifically told them not to and they wouldn't betray my trust. It's about telling people you trust."

"I trust no one," Mark says.

"Awesome. Makes me optimistic about our future."

He laughs. "All right, Brendan, have a good night. I hope you liked my stalker gesture."

"Loved it."

We give each other an official good-night kiss before he heads back to his car.

CHAPTER THIRTEEN

Mark and I have been dating for about six weeks now, but we haven't done anything past kissing. Being sexual with a guy is foreign to both of us, so we wanted to take things slowly. Yes, it's been hard to resist going further, but it will all be worth it this weekend. Mark's parents are taking his sister to a soccer tournament in Columbus, and they will be staying there Friday night.

That means Mark and I will finally have a whole night to ourselves alone. And we both agree that we've waited long enough to get physical. Of course we won't have sex. I'm staying steadfast in my decision to wait, at least for now, but just about everything else is on the table.

I'd like nothing more than to stay overnight at Mark's, holding him in my arms while we sleep. I even considered telling my mom that I'd be out on the east side tonight and might just sleep at a friend's there, but I realized it would only invite more suspicion. Besides, the chances she'd say yes are slim. Oh well. This Friday will still be amazing.

The days leading up to the big day went *painfully* slow. It was all I could think about. Kissing Mark gets me ramped up enough. Going beyond that? My brain is exploding imagining it.

I'm also getting nervous about it all. What if I'm bad at everything I try? What if it's awkward? Fortunately, after arriving at his house and seeing his face, my nerves calm.

"You're early," Mark says to me after opening the door. "Eager to get over here?"

I can't help but notice how good he looks. He always looks put-together, but tonight he looks extra spiffy, wearing a fitted gray T-shirt with his hair perfectly tousled.

We get some pizza delivered and relax in his living room while catching each other up on our week. For the first time, since no one is home at his house, we aren't exiled to the basement. Every touch and kiss is foreplay, getting me more and more excited for what's going to come later tonight.

"Guess what," I say to him as we eat our dinner.

"What?"

"My sister's pregnant."

"I knew that."

"Sorry, my *other* sister."

He laughs. "That's awesome. So this will be your third niece or nephew?"

"Yep."

"Do you like kids?" he asks.

"I love babies and am great with them. Once they reach, like, age four, they tend to annoy me. They just have an attitude, right?"

"I'm the opposite. Babies are too fragile for me. I always worry they're going to fall and get hurt or choke on something. Once they get a little older, I can do more stuff with them like play games and sports."

"So together we'd make perfect parents."

He smiles. "Do you want kids?"

"Yeah. You?"

"Yeah. But how would you?" he asks.

"I don't know. I haven't really thought about it."

"So, when you pictured your future before you realized you're gay, was it different?"

"What do you mean?"

"Like, when you were younger, didn't you picture yourself marrying a girl?"

"Oh. I guess so."

"So then once you came out, did you just swap the girl out for a guy? But the picture in your mind stayed the same?"

I think about it for a few seconds. "Yeah, exactly. If I want to get married and have kids, that's what I'm going to do, regardless of whether I'm gay or straight. Why do you ask?"

"It's just cool how simple things are in your brain. When it comes to all this, my thoughts go all over the place. For you, nothing big seems to have changed."

After we finish our food, it's time for the main event. Mark takes my hand and leads me up to his bedroom, stopping every few feet to give me a kiss. What I've been fantasizing about for weeks is about to come to fruition.

Once in his room, Mark lies down on his bed and pulls me on top of him. We slowly start to kiss, barely touching our lips to each other.

"Kissing on my bed for the first time," he says.

"Much better than a couch."

Our kisses become more intense, our breathing heavier. I roll over on my back and pull him on top of me. I move my hands from his face to the back of his head where I grab his hair, perhaps harder than I planned.

He slides his lips across my left cheek until they land on my neck. He kisses it gently before moving to my ear. When I feel like I can't take it anymore, I grab his face and bring his lips back to mine.

While kissing him, I tug at his shirt and pull it up over his head, our lips coming apart for only a second before meeting again. I throw it across the room and grip his back. Our lips part, and I kiss his chest, gently licking his nipples before moving down his stomach. I stop at the top of his pants and slide my tongue back and forth just above his waist. I hear him moan and enjoy teasing him, knowing that the teasing is only temporary tonight.

He pulls away as he slides his body down the bed and hikes my shirt up to reveal my stomach. It's time for payback. He proceeds to kiss my stomach, hitting my ticklish spots he's discovered over the past few weeks. He moves his mouth up my stomach and chest, bringing my shirt up with him until it is scrunched at my neck. I pull it up over my arms and head, tossing it in the same direction that I threw his.

What happens next feels better than I could have ever imagined. After we're done, Mark and I roll onto our backs and catch our breath. My body needs a minute to recover. He leans over and kisses me.

"I'm speechless," I finally say.

He laughs. "You're so sexy." I shake my head and point to him.

After a few minutes, our paralysis wears off. We get dressed in our comfy clothes and take advantage of the fact that we have his bed to lie in for the rest of the night. We snuggle up together as he holds me in his arms, which honestly feels just as good as what we just experienced.

"All right, I have to ask," I say later in the night as my head rests on his chest. "Be honest."

"Well, your ear is resting on my heart right now, so if it starts to race, you'll know I'm lying."

"Good. I'm a lie detector. So, what you and I just did…how does that compare to one of your past hook-ups with a girl?" He bursts into laughter. "Mark, I feel your heart beating faster. Don't lie to me."

"I haven't even said anything yet. What happened with you just now was more intense than any other physical experience I've ever had." I smile, but I'm not sure he can see my face. "How's my heart rate?"

"Steady," I respond.

"See, I'd never lie to you. Want to know the coolest thing? That was the *first* time you and I have done anything together. It's only going to get hotter from here."

"You think?" I ask, turning my head to look up at him.

"Trust me. Your imagination is probably running wild with ideas. I know how dirty your mind is."

"No. I'm innocent, remember?"

"Right," Mark says. "That's what I thought when I first met you. I was afraid I'd say something that would offend you or something. Then I came to know the truth."

"Well, I think I was a little repressed. Hormones raging and all. Tonight they were released…literally."

Mark laughs. "What am I going to do with you?"

"You know what I really like?" I say. "How you appreciate my weirdness and goofiness. I've always been myself around you and have never felt judged."

"Well, the truth is I think you're a total dork, but it makes me really attracted to you. And I think it brings out *my* goofy side, which I don't normally express with my friends."

"I love that side of you." After a few seconds of silence, I have a thought. "Don't you wish we could just have privacy like this all the time? It would be so much easier."

"I know. Believe me, I know. Until then…" He grabs my face and kisses me.

CHAPTER FOURTEEN

Kelly and Reese are turning eighteen this week (even their *birthdays* are practically the same), so my friends and I are going to a dinner for them tonight. Because I'm not able to see Mark, he and I decide to get lunch in the afternoon followed by a little shopping.

I suck at picking out clothes. He, on the other hand, looks good in every single article of clothing he owns, so I'm pretty much going to buy whatever he tells me to buy.

Before shopping, we decide to go to a Mediterranean restaurant not too far from my house. It's part of a larger outdoor shopping center/restaurant haven.

Mark and I walk into the restaurant, side by side, but before I can tell the hostess that we would like a table for two, I hear a familiar voice.

"Um, Brendan…"

I turn to my right to find Natalie and her mom sitting at a table. Oh no. I've always been worried about running into someone I know while out with Mark. I guess I expected it to be an acquaintance or a relative to whom I could quickly say hi, choose whether to introduce Mark, and then move on. I've never played out this scenario with one of my best friends.

I try to make my face look as if I didn't just get caught. I briefly turn to Mark to find that he isn't as successful in accomplishing this with his.

"Natalie, what's up?" I force a slight laugh. Mark stays silent but smiles at her. "Hi, Mrs. Suarez," I say to Natalie's mom.

Natalie's confused look remains on her face as she asks, "What are you guys doing here?" What she really means to say is, *Why are you two hanging out alone together?* I take care of all the talking while Mark stands by.

"Oh, I was bored at home and decided I want to do some shopping, and Mark has to buy something for his mom's birthday, so we decided to go together."

Where did that come from? I don't even know when Mark's mom's birthday is, but luckily Natalie doesn't either so my lie isn't obvious. Despite trying to sound casual, she's definitely still not convinced.

I choose not to continue my rambling and instead ask, "You're going to the dinner tonight, right?"

I make eye contact with the hostess, who has returned to her stand. I hold two fingers up so we have an excuse to exit the conversation.

"Yeah, I'll be there," Natalie says.

"Okay, cool. I'll see you then. Good seeing you, Mrs. Suarez."

Mark and I speed walk to our table, which, fortunately, isn't near Natalie's.

"Crap, crap, crap," I whisper with a fake slight smile on my face to appear unfazed as we sit down.

"This is bad, isn't it?"

"No," I say, trying to reassure him and myself. "I just have to make sure I know what I'm going to say tonight when she asks me about this.

"Okay, you and I are friends," I continue. "She knows that. I just need to play it off like it's not unusual for us to hang out one-on-one. I'll explain that we see each other a good amount at school and have become closer."

"Okay. Don't overexplain, though." I can tell he's worried.

"I know. I wish I had never told her I have feelings for you. Otherwise, she wouldn't be as suspicious."

"Wait, did you ever tell her that you confessed your feelings to me...and that I rejected you?" he says with an innocent smile.

"Actually, no. Why?"

"Okay, then you need to. Tell her you moved on from me a while ago because you realized there was no hope once I rejected you. Then—"

"Can you stop saying the word 'reject'? I still have a complex from that night," I say jokingly.

He cracks a smile before continuing. "But seriously, then it makes sense that we're friends. We decided that we still like hanging out with each other, but you understood that nothing romantic would ever happen with us."

"Okay." I'm not sure his explanation would convince Natalie and especially Chris, but he thinks it's great, so I don't argue. Besides, he doesn't need to worry about this. I'm the one who will be dealing with it tonight.

"Also," Mark says, "my mom's birthday?!"

I laugh. "No idea. I panicked."

❖

That night, I arrive at the restaurant a little late, but immediately spot Reese and her tiara sitting with the others.

"I'm confused," Natalie says as I sit down. "I've never arrived somewhere before you. What's happening?"

"I know. This feels so unnatural."

"Did your shopping trip go long?" she asks.

"Yeah, actually. I lost track of time. And the stores were crowded." I wait for more prying but she doesn't say anything.

Chris, however, jumps right in. "Brendan, I heard you and Mark had a little lunch date today."

"Oh, yeah," I say. Until he asks me a question, I'm not going to give him any more information. Like Mark told me, I shouldn't overexplain. Liars always give themselves away by offering up too many details.

"What's going on there?" he asks in a somewhat jealous tone.

"What do you mean?"

"Brendan, come on," Natalie chimes in. "A couple months ago you were head over heels for him, and now you're hanging out with him one-on-one, which we had no idea about."

I give a slight laugh. Time for Mark's plan. "Okay, I didn't tell you this—well, Kara knows—but on New Year's Eve I told Mark how I felt about him, and he straight up rejected me." Mark's favorite word again. "But he was really nice about it and still wanted to be friends, so we are. I moved on. Like you said, that was a couple months ago. Besides, today was one of the few times I've hung out with him alone."

"I'm going to need to hear the details of that New Year's Eve story later," Natalie says. "But staying on this topic, isn't it strange that he knows you have feelings for him, and don't pretend that you still don't, but he wants to hang out with you alone? Most straight guys wouldn't do that."

Kelly, Reese, and Kara have a lull in their conversation, so their eyes turn to Natalie and me.

"I agree with you," I tell Natalie. "I expected Mark to keep his distance because I made things awkward by telling him."

"What's going on?" Kelly asks. "What did you tell him?"

Chris gives a quick recap to bring them up to speed and to bring in more people whom I now have to go up against.

Kelly gives her take on the situation. "So you told him you liked him, and since then you've gotten to the point where he asks you out for lunch and a shopping spree? He likes you." Sometimes she can be so matter-of-fact with her simplification of things. It's annoying because this time she's right.

"I wish he liked me," I say. "Believe me. But I don't think he does. He doesn't flirt or anything. I think he just likes having me as a friend. Just like he's friends with Chris."

Kara comes to my rescue. "And Chris, you said he loves attention, right? So I'm sure he was flattered that Brendan liked him. It wouldn't push him away."

Chris ignores her and keeps digging. "You said this is *one* of the only times you've hung out with him alone. So, when else did you hang out?"

"Oh, well on New Year's we got dinner alone. You knew that. And I've gotten food after school with him and stuff."

"See, now I'm wondering if that mystery guy you went on a date with last month is Mark," Natalie says.

"Wait, what?" Chris says.

"Thank you for bringing that up, Natalie," I say, partly annoyed that she's telling everyone about that, partly annoyed that her suspicions are dead on.

"Who did you go out with?" Chris asks.

"I can't say because he's not out. And it doesn't matter because that was *one* date. It didn't go anywhere."

"Does he go to Xavier?" Chris asks.

"It doesn't matter. That date was nothing."

"I still feel like you're hiding something from us," Natalie says. Apparently I'm not too convincing. I'm too tense. This is a problem with being an open book. Once you start to be secretive, people notice.

"What do you mean?" I smile, trying to look more relaxed.

"I don't know. I just think normal Brendan would be so excited if Mark asked him to hang out."

"I think *I* asked *him* to hang out today."

"Okay, fine. Then you'd be excited that he said yes and you'd run and tell us."

"It's not that big a deal. I mean, I'm sure I still have some lingering feelings for him, but I don't think about it because I already did all I could with that situation. I told him how I felt. So even if he were gay or did like me, he'd never admit it."

"Well, if he does, you have to tell us," Chris says.

I feign a laugh. "Okay, deal. But he'd probably tell *you* before he told *me*."

The questioning stops when the waiter comes to take our order.

After ordering, Reese, who has stayed silent throughout the conversation, changes the subject. If she suspects I'm lying, she also respects that I want to keep this private, so she has not contributed to the inquisition. She's always been good at letting people do their own thing and not getting involved in things that don't concern her.

"Okay, enough of that," she says. "Who's everyone taking to prom?"

"Natalie's taking me," Chris says.

"Yes, I'm taking a gay guy," Natalie replies. "It's my responsibility and destiny."

"Who's taking Brendan?" Kelly asks.

"I call him," Reese says. "Unless I can convince Steve to go with me."

"Who?" Kara and I say in unison.

"This guy I work with. He's so hot. He has a pierced lip, his waist is smaller than mine, and he smells like a vanilla car freshener."

"Hot," Natalie says.

"Okay, when will you know?" Kelly asks. "Because if you don't take Brendan, I will."

"Give me two weeks."

"Forget about *our* prom," Natalie says. "Let's talk about prom at Xavier. Brendan, who are you taking, because I *have* to go."

"Chris can take you," Reese says.

"Reese, I'm a junior," Chris says. "Don't make it worse."

She laughs. "Oh my gosh, I wasn't thinking. Brendan, you can take Natalie. Kelly and I will find dates."

"Speak for yourself," Kelly says.

"Let's figure it out when we're closer to the day," I say.

"Wait, Brendan, you can't take Natalie," Chris says. "Aren't you taking Mark?"

"You're funny," I say to him. Clearly they won't be forgetting about this any time soon.

"Kara, are you and Andrew going to be in our prom group if we go?" Kelly asks.

"I don't know. I don't know what his friends are doing."

"Are you kidding?" Natalie says. "You might not sit at our table?"

"It's *his* prom. I don't know."

"Well, I think he should let you go with your closest friends," Natalie says. "He probably doesn't even care about the dance."

"I'll be with all of you for *our* prom."

"That's not the same," Natalie says. "You know prom is a bigger deal at Xavier."

"All right, well, I'm not going to tell Andrew what to do for *his* dance."

"Of course you won't, because that would require you to stand up to him."

"Oh boy," Kelly says.

I interject, trying to defuse the situation. I don't want Kara to get upset, and I hate the awkwardness. "Natalie, I don't get it. You don't think Kara can stand up for herself when it comes to Andrew?"

"I think she often does what *he* wants to do and is forced to hang out with his friends," Natalie explains.

I look over at Kara, who gives an eye roll before saying, "I'm ready to change the subject." Fortunately, the conversation doesn't ruin the night.

❖

After dinner, I call Natalie so that I can talk to her one-on-one. I hate when two of my best friends fight. I want to hear both sides of the story, but I also feel protective if one of them attacks the other.

"Hi," she says after picking up.

"Okay, please fill me in. I know we're not a fan of Andrew, but I don't think he treats Kara badly or anything."

"Brendan, how many times have you hung out with them together?"

"Not nearly as much as you," I admit.

Natalie and Kara are members of the flag corps team at my school while Andrew is part of the band. Through practice, games and even band camp, Natalie has definitely spent a lot more time with them than I have.

"Exactly," she says. "I've watched them since they started dating a year ago. When she's around him, she's not herself. She's much more self-conscious and awkward."

"Okay, but is that because she's around him *and you* at the same time, so she doesn't know how to balance?"

"Balance what? It shouldn't matter who she's around. She should act herself, especially around her best friend and boyfriend. It's not like we're strangers."

"True. So how do you think she acts when it's just her and him?"

"Who knows?"

"All I know is she says that she's happy with him."

"She *says* that."

"I understand if you're concerned, but it comes off as you being mean and hard on her."

"I just think that she tends to put Andrew before us," Natalie says.

"See, I disagree with you there. We see her pretty much every weekend."

"I'm not talking about just the weekends. If you saw them as much as I do, you'd think the same thing."

"All right, that's fair. Agree to disagree."

"And look," she says, "if I were in your shoes, I probably wouldn't think she puts him in front of us. But I'm going off *my* experiences here."

"I hear you."

I'm not going to let Natalie's experience affect my view of Kara, but it *is* eye opening to hear her reasons for being annoyed. As Natalie said, she can only base her opinions off *her* experiences, and I can only base them off mine. It's tough because I just want all of us to get along, but I guess it's normal for there to be strains in friendships at some point.

❖

The next morning, it doesn't take long for Mark to call. Halfway through breakfast, my phone rings.

"Hey, Kara, can I call you back soon?" I answer. He knows that if I call him by another name, my mom is around. About ten minutes later, I head up to my room and call Mark back. I'm a little worried my mom will become suspicious with these private calls, but I even take phone calls from my friends in privacy, so it's nothing new.

"Hi," Mark answers.

"What up?"

"Oh, nothing. Just wondering how last night went."

I sugarcoat my recap of the story. I can tell that our run-in with Natalie combined with Chris's growing suspicions have made Mark increasingly worried that we're going to be found out. I don't want to add to his stress, but I also don't want to lie to him.

"So do you think they believed you?" Mark asks.

"I think so. I tried to make it seem like they were crazy for thinking that, and that I *wish* what they thought were true, but it's not."

"Okay."

"But I'm not going to lie. They're still going to be suspicious."

"I know."

"Are you okay?" I ask. "You sound worried."

He sighs. "I don't know. I keep thinking that the longer we date, the harder it's going to be to hide it from everyone. I don't want it to get any worse."

"I know. Well, the good news is no one in *your* life is suspicious besides Chris. Just *my* friends."

"Yeah," he says, still sounding dejected.

I try to lighten the mood with sarcasm. "So until your soccer friends start grilling you about me, you're in the clear."

"Brendan, can we be serious for a minute?"

"Yeah."

"I don't think you understand the difference between our situations here. You've already come to terms with the fact that you're gay. You've told your closest friends. If they found out that you and I are dating, it would make your life *easier* because you wouldn't have to hide it anymore. Me? I accepted that I have feelings for you, but as for whether I'm gay, I don't know. I've had no desire to answer that question.

"So right now," he continues, "yes, I'm really worried that someone is going to find out about us because it will then spread at our school, which will no doubt lead to my friends. Once that happens, the question of my sexuality that I haven't answered yet will be answered by everyone else. I'd be gay."

So far our relationship has been so easy. We're always in a happy mood when we're around each other, and our outside worries go away. This is the first time I've heard him really distraught.

He's absolutely right; our situations are very different. He's not ready to go through what I've already faced this past year.

"I get where you're coming from," I say. "But let's be honest. This probably won't be the last time we're going to have a close call." Then a question enters my mind that I have to ask. "Do you ever question whether you want to continue dating?"

I was expecting a swift "no" but instead, there's silence on the end of the line.

"Honestly, it's crossed my mind," he finally says. "I haven't given it any serious thought or anything. You know how much I like you. It's just…I don't know how to say this…"

"You can be honest." His extended pauses indicate that he's debating whether to deliver a blow.

"I know that I'm not ready for anyone to know about us," he says. "So if that's what's going to happen if we keep dating, I don't know if it's a good idea." After a pause, he asks, "Are you there?"

"Yes."

"I'm not saying I want to end things," he quickly adds. "I'm telling you what's been on my mind."

"I know. And you can be honest with me about this stuff anytime. I can handle it. What you're saying makes sense. I guess what I want to say is that it would suck if this ends. You and I get along so well."

"I know."

"And I don't want to pressure you, I promise, but can you even let yourself imagine being okay with people knowing about us? Or is it an 'absolutely not' sort of thing? Because what if we're still dating in six months? Or a year? Do you think you'll want to be open about this part of your life?"

"No," he simply says. I wait for him to elaborate. "I'm getting anxiety thinking about that right now. I haven't let myself think about what my life would be like if people knew."

"Fair enough." It's not what I want to hear, but I knew what I was getting into when we started dating. I can hope things will be different someday, but I have to accept that they may not.

"Okay," I continue. "Let's think about where we go from here. Natalie and Chris are a little suspicious. Kara already knows but won't tell anyone, and my mom doesn't even know who you are, so she's not a legitimate worry either. As for my other friends, they don't care enough to keep an eye on us. Trust me. So when we hang out, maybe we should pick more random locations where it's a lot less likely that we'll run into anyone."

"Yes. And we can hang out at my house whenever."

"Are you sure?"

"Yeah. Maybe I should be more worried about my parents, but I'm not. My main concern is my friends finding out."

"Okay, cool. I'm fine cutting back on the public outings. And we should give each other code names in our phones. Not kidding."

He laughs. "You sound so excited about that."

"I mean, that's pretty fun, right? Although I guess renaming you 'Sexy' defeats the purpose of being discreet. I'll think of something else."

"Oh, Brendan," he sighs. "Thanks for being understanding. And thanks for being willing to put on a charade with all of your friends."

"Look, there's been some crap we've had to deal with since we started dating, but I'm really happy with you, which is all that matters."

"Aw," he says.

"Seriously."

"Well, that makes me feel a lot better about everything."

Although my conversation with Mark ends well, I'm still worried he's a flight risk. I may have made him feel better today, but what if we have another close call? How much more is he willing to put up with before he decides that I'm not worth the risk?

I'm the happiest I've ever been in my life, and a large part of that is due to him. Don't get me wrong; I was happy before Mark, but having him as a boyfriend has added a new layer to my happiness. I know I should try to imagine my life without him in case he and I don't work out for whatever reason, but my brain won't let me think like that. Not yet, at least.

If Mark and I broke up for reasons of incompatibility, I would be able to accept that. But breaking up because someone in my life might find out and tell one of his friends? That would be incredibly frustrating.

CHAPTER FIFTEEN

The following week brings a noticeable shift in Mark's behavior. He and I barely talk, and he sounds so closed off when we do. We are hanging out this Thursday, so I decide to give him some space and time to think until then. It's as if his worries are land mines that could go off at any moment, depending on how much pressure I put on him.

After school on Wednesday, he calls me.

"Hey, Brendan, what's up?"

"Nothing, just doing homework."

"Nice. So listen, I know we're supposed to hang out tomorrow, but my soccer team is planning to go to dinner after our game. I feel like I should probably go."

"Okay. What time do you think you'll be done?"

"I probably won't be back on the west side until like ten."

"Gotcha."

"Yeah, I'm sorry," he says. "But you're still able to hang out Saturday?"

"Yeah."

"Okay, cool."

"Well, what are you doing tonight?" I ask. "Can you hang out?"

"I kind of have a lot of school work to do."

"Okay. Is everything okay? I shouldn't read into this..."

"No, I'm good," he says.

"All right, then I guess I will talk to you…before Saturday?"

"Yeah, of course."

"All right, have fun."

Well, that was brief. My anxiety isn't going away anytime soon. I was hoping to get some reassurance from Mark, but with his last-minute cancellation, I don't think things are okay.

❖

Thankfully, a few days later, Mark keeps our Saturday plans to hang out at his house. I'm still shocked that his parents haven't caught on. Maybe they have, and we're being totally naïve. Regardless of what I think, he is convinced we have nothing to worry about and being in his home is safer than anywhere in public.

With that said, I convince him to go see a movie with me before we head to his house so his parents think that we have some semblance of a social life. Besides, a dark theater is almost as safe as his basement.

We manage to see the movie without being seen by anyone we know and get back to his house at about nine-thirty. His parents are already upstairs for the night. Good.

I was worried how Mark would behave tonight considering it's the first time we've hung out since his mini freak-out, and he hasn't said much this past week. To be honest, the night started out weird. We just weren't clicking like we usually do. Fortunately, by the time we get to his house, we slip into our normal groove. His paranoia has faded and he is his usual self.

"Explain the riddle again," he says. "I was distracted." In the car I told him about a brainteaser I read years ago. Unfortunately, I never found out the answer to it. I always tell people that it will just frustrate them once I say it, but he's convinced that he can figure it out.

"Okay," I say as I open his cupboard to see what junk food he has. "You're walking along a road, trying to get downtown. Then there's a fork in the road. The road splits into two, okay?"

"Yes, I know what a fork in the road is."

"Jerk. Okay, so now you don't know which of the two roads will take you downtown." He nods with an intense stare on his face as I continue. "In front of each road is a man. One man always lies and one always tells the truth. But you don't know which man is which. Funyuns!" I say after spotting them in the cupboard. "My favorite."

"Brendan," he says, trying to hide his smile.

"Okay, you can only ask one man one question in order to figure out which road will take you downtown. So, what question do you ask and to whom?"

He scrunches his forehead and stays silent for about five seconds while I start eating the Funyuns.

"This is complicated," he finally says.

"Uh, yeah. There are so many layers to it. Which road is right? Who's telling the truth? What question do you ask?"

"And you seriously don't know the answer to this?"

"Seriously."

"I hate you right now," he says.

I laugh. "So frustrating, right?"

"Do you have any gum?"

"Yeah, here you go," I say, pulling a pack out of my back pocket.

"Oh, it's not for me. I just want to make sure I don't have to make out with onion breath tonight."

"I'm about to punch you," I say.

"Why don't you pin me down instead?"

"Oh, I was going to do that anyway. Look, I'm done with these." I close the Funyuns bag and put it back in the cupboard.

"No. Take them down. I was just messing with you."

I shake my head. "I'm done anyway."

"In that case," he says before taking my hand and leading the way down the basement. I pull the gum out again and quickly pop a piece into my mouth.

After sitting down on the couch and turning on the TV, Mark says, "With one question, you somehow have to figure out which guy is telling the truth *and* which road will take you downtown."

"I know which road will take you downtown," I say, grabbing his shirt and pulling him in for a kiss.

"Don't distract me." I start to kiss him. "Okay, you can distract me," he whispers.

After a few seconds, I pull back. "All right, can I talk to you about something?"

"I know," he says. I look at him, perplexed. "I was weird this week."

"Yeah. Up until an hour ago, you were not yourself."

"I'm sorry. I had a lot of thoughts running through my brain."

"I figured. Mark, you have no one to talk to when it comes to us except for one person—me. Even if you think something you say is going to make me upset, you should tell me. I can handle it. Otherwise, you'll make yourself crazy by keeping everything bottled up."

"You're right."

"So do you want to talk about it?" I ask.

"It's the same stuff we talked about last weekend. Nothing new. I'd rather enjoy my time with you tonight instead of talking about my worries. It's easy when it's the two of us, but I have a lot of time to think when I'm away from you."

"So next time you have doubts or worries, focus on the times we've spent together and think about how you'd just *die* if I weren't a part of your life."

He laughs before giving me a kiss. Nothing too exciting is on TV, so after a couple minutes of channel surfing, we start making out. We start off on our sides, facing each other, but it doesn't take long for me to get on top of him.

I continue to kiss him when I suddenly hear a gasp from a few feet away. I look to the bottom of the staircase to find Eva staring at us, her face in shock. I quickly get off Mark, but before he and I can say anything, she darts back up the stairs.

All this time, I was worried that Mark's parents would find out about us. I never thought about his sister.

Mark is still staring at the staircase. The look on his face is one that I've never seen before. His stare is blank, his face void of any emotion. I know I have to say something, but I don't know what.

Finally, I break the silence, still not knowing what words will come out. "Mark…it will be okay." My words snap him out of his daze and he instantly sits up, his eyes now staring at the ground. "If you talk to her and explain…"

"Oh my gosh," he finally says quietly. "Brendan, you need to leave." He looks at me for the first time since seeing Eva. "I can't handle this right now." His eyes go back to the ground.

My gut tells me not to fight it so I say, "Okay." I think about rubbing my hand on his back to comfort him, but I don't think he wants me anywhere close to him right now. We both stand up and walk upstairs. Eva is nowhere to be seen.

"I promise it will be okay," I whisper to him when we get to the front door. "Please call or text me tonight." He nods.

I know that nothing I say right now will help. If anything, my presence is hurting things.

The moment Eva saw us replays in my mind on the way home. How did we not hear her walk down? How did we not hear the basement door open? The TV must have been too loud.

Then the big question hits me: How have I not once worried about Eva finding out about us? She's sixteen. If anyone in Mark's family were to figure it out, it would be her.

I wonder if she had suspicions before tonight. Maybe she did and kept them to herself because she likes me and was happy that Mark and I are together. No. Her face tonight was pure shock. Thank God he and I were just kissing. It could have been much worse.

I stay up late that night, waiting for something from Mark. As if I could have fallen asleep anyway. By one in the morning, I give up. I think about calling him but decide to give him space and let him sleep. Hopefully we'll feel better in the morning.

By two the next day, I still hadn't heard from him. I pick up the phone and call him. He doesn't answer. I try to distract myself while I wait for him to call me back.

A couple of hours later, my phone finally rings.

"Hi, Mark."

"Hey."

"Are you okay?"

"Um…no, not really."

"What happened?" I ask. "Did you talk to Eva?"

"Yeah, I did."

"Is she going to tell your parents?"

"No, I don't think so. She said she wouldn't."

"Good."

"Brendan…" Oh no. I know what he's going to say. "I don't think I can do this anymore." I try to think of something to say that will convince him otherwise, but I can't form a thought. "It's just too much. I didn't know what to say to Eva. If we keep dating, who knows who will find out next? My parents? I would have no idea what to say to them."

"You could tell them the truth," I say, trying not to sound as frustrated as I am. "I know that sounds ridiculous to you but, Mark, you're happy with me. *If* your parents were to find out about us, maybe they would be okay with it.

"Look," I continue, "the last time we talked about this, you said that our situations are different, and you're right. I'm not denying that. But my gosh, Mark. You're preventing yourself from being happy." I hear my voice get louder as I keep talking.

"You're right, Brendan, I am. But I didn't know what the hell to say to Eva." His volume matches mine. "She asked me if I'm gay and I…didn't know what to say."

"You say that you don't know because that's the truth, but what you do know is that you like me. That's all that matters right now."

"No."

"Yes."

"I wish it were that simple, but it's not."

"It *can* be if you stop letting outside distractions get in the way."

"My sister walking in on us is not a distraction. It's a big deal. Look, the bottom line is what just happened with Eva…I can't imagine that happening with my parents or friends or cousins or anyone else in my life. I'm not ready for that. I can't risk it. I'm sorry."

"I knew this was going to happen," I say quietly, admitting defeat. "I knew that you were going to reach your breaking point and give up."

"Brendan, put yourself in my shoes."

"I *have*. For the past couple months I've constantly been looking out for you and trying to keep our relationship under wraps. I've also been blowing off my friends for you because I knew we couldn't all hang out together."

"I know. And I'm sorry about that."

"I'm not saying that I don't understand. I'm just annoyed and frustrated, and when it finally hits me that we're no longer together..."

"I know."

I feel my eyes swell, but I don't want him to hear me cry. I never let anyone see me cry. Heck, I never cry. "All right, I'm going to go."

"I'm sorry, Brendan."

After hanging up, I let it all out. I can't remember the last time I cried, but it makes me feel better, as if I'm releasing all of my frustration and sadness.

Our relationship has been nothing but great. Even our breakup conversation was mature and respectful. I always hoped that his feelings for me would be stronger than his fear of our being found out. I guess that's not the case.

I stay in my room for the night, hiding my emotions from my mom. After a light dinner, I go to bed early, hoping that sleep will help. I normally hate Mondays, but I'm looking forward to tomorrow so that I can get back into a routine that will hopefully distract me.

CHAPTER SIXTEEN

The next week is a blur. I go through school and rehearsal, but I don't feel present at all. I don't have enough energy to fake a smile, and my friends immediately notice. They ask me if everything is okay; I say yes. They ask me if something is wrong; I say no. They tell me that I seem really down; I tell them that I'm just tired.

I'm thankful to go through the entire school week without seeing Mark. Looking down while walking through the halls helped. Maybe I even passed him without knowing.

My mom notices my shift in attitude too. "What's wrong with you?" she asks me exactly one week after the incident.

"Nothing."

"Are you mad at me?"

"Nope."

"Well then, what's going on?"

"I'm fine."

"Are you going out with your friends tonight?"

I stayed in the night before and have been lounging around the house the whole day. I really should try to be social tonight. I can't remember the last time I stayed in on a Friday *and* Saturday.

"Maybe," I answer.

I can tell my mom is still concerned, but she doesn't push any farther. My sadness mixes with anger as I realize that having to hide my relationship with Mark from my mom added significant strain and stress. Mark wasn't ready to tell his parents about us, but after meeting them, I honestly think that they might have accepted our relationship. Had my mom found out about us, it would have been even more bad news.

I start to think that our relationship was doomed from the start. No couple can last if they have to hide it from virtually everyone in their lives, especially when they still *live* with people from whom they have to hide it.

Someone was going to find out. Some of my friends were already on our trail. Who knows how much longer they would have needed before they got their proof?

Although I'm frustrated with Mark for ending things, I also feel bad for him. He wasn't ready for anyone to know about us and now his only sister knows. I don't know whether she'll keep her word and not tell her parents, but my guess is she will.

A few hours later, after agreeing to go to Kara's house tonight to hang out, I manage to shower and look presentable—at least not *totally* depressed. By the time I arrive at Kara's, I'm actually feeling slightly better. If anyone is going to help improve my mood, it's her and my other friends.

Since Kara is the only one I'm able to talk to about Mark, I arrive at her place early to give us some time before the others arrive. Of course we spoke on the phone earlier this week, but it's nice to have an in-person therapy session with her.

She does her best to reassure me everything will be okay. She helps me understand this wasn't my fault. I kept my loyalty to him and did my best to be discreet. What happened was out of my control, so there's no blame on me.

"Honestly, Brendan, I was curious how long you were going to be able to keep your relationship hidden," she says. "You two have too many people who are close to you. Someone was bound to find out eventually."

"You're right. We had to keep that secret bottled up, and each time someone became suspicious, whether it was Chris seeing my text to Mark or Natalie seeing us at lunch, the secret got shaken up. Keeping the lid on it became harder."

"And with Eva spotting you two, the pressure finally became too much."

I nod. "Kaboom."

I feel a lot better after talking with her, but I have one question that I feel pathetic even asking.

"There's no way he'd be willing to date again." I say it as a statement, but Kara knows that I'm looking for her opinion.

"I don't know, Brendan. He took a chance with you and went with his feelings. After this, I think he's going to use his brain. But I don't know. You know him a lot better than I do."

"I think you're right. He's probably kicking himself for ever dating me in the first place."

"No."

"No, I'm not saying that in a self-deprecating way. But now that his sister knows, he probably wishes he had never told me he liked me. If he had just played it safe and suppressed his feelings, he would have never had to deal with this mess."

She nods in understanding. "So have you not talked to him *at all* since you broke up?"

"No."

"Like, not even a text?"

"You know I hate texting. And Mark and I didn't text that much. If we did, it would be during school. Otherwise, we would just call each other. Would you have ever predicted that I'd be this torn up over a breakup? I'm usually so emotionless."

"I know. Hearing you cry on the phone this week was so weird. I had never heard or seen you cry in my life."

"I needed a release. The breakup combined with the issues I've had with my mom combined with the stress of trying to keep everything a secret…"

"Combined with the stress of trying to pick a college," she says.

"It's been a crazy couple of months."

I switch topics because I'm sure Kara can only take so much of my analyzing. She starts to tell me about her week, but the doorbell rings. Kelly has arrived.

I keep my spirits up the rest of the night, apparently convincing Kelly and the others that I'm okay. Hanging out and laughing with everyone helps more than I expected. I miss Mark a lot, but I'm fortunate to have such a great group of friends.

I try to spend the next few weeks with a smile on my face and a positive attitude. It's time to get back to my normal self. Plus, I need to keep my spirits and energy high because I have a busy couple of weeks coming up.

Next weekend is our musical, which means long nights of rehearsal all week. Then, two days after closing night, tennis season starts. Also not too far off is attending prom at St. Mary's with Reese. She wasn't able to convince her work crush to go with her. Mark will also be going with one of his friends. Let's just say I'm not exactly looking forward to it. Regardless, I'm hoping my busy schedule will keep my mind off him.

❖

I've made some progress in forgetting about Mark, but I'm not as successful as I had hoped. The truth is I still miss him. I don't understand why I can't get past it. I know I've never been in a relationship before, but if someone had asked me a few months ago if it would be easy for me to move on after a breakup with someone, I would have said absolutely. Before I met Mark, I was perfectly happy with my solitude. I like my alone time and not having to answer to anyone. Yet here I am, feeling like something is now missing from my life, a void that only Mark can fill.

What's that expression? *It's better to have loved and lost than never to have loved at all?* That's crap. Then you're just stuck with the memories of when you used to be happy. Memories that are so vivid, you wonder if they'll ever fade at all.

I still haven't talked to Mark since our phone conversation the day after the Eva incident. If he were to reach out to me at some point, today would be the day. It's my eighteenth birthday. I'm not expecting anything, but I can't lie—a part of me is hoping for some form of communication from him. It's false hope, I know.

Today is also the last day of rehearsal for the school musical before opening night this weekend. Man, it's flown by. Fortunately, the rehearsal goes really well. I've been part of multiple shows where the cast does not feel ready going into the final week of rehearsals. For this show, however, we all feel great and are more than ready to finally get in front of an audience.

I walk out to my car after rehearsal and see that it has been vandalized with spray paint, signs, and glitter. My friends have been here.

"You're 18! You can finally buy lottery tickets!" one sign reads. Another one has "Happy Birthday" written in huge letters with about a dozen signatures from friends and acquaintances at the bottom. Everywhere I look I see reminders of why I have the best friends.

By the time I get home, I'm starving. Fortunately, my mom already has a steak cooking for me. A few minutes later, as I am about to take my first bite, I hear my front door open, followed by multiple footsteps. What the heck? I see that it's my usual crew of friends. The five of them are dressed in all black with pantyhose over their heads.

"Let's go!" Natalie shouts at me, wanting me to get up and follow them. Apparently I'm being kidnapped. I'm excited to see where they are going to take me, but my stomach refuses to let me get up.

"You guys, I am *so* hungry right now. Please let me eat something, and then I'm all yours."

"Are you kidding me?" Natalie says.

"Ten minutes. I'll eat fast."

They take off their pantyhose and sit down at the table to watch me eat. I scarf down my food and allow them to blindfold me before pushing me into Kelly's car while I hear a Kelly Clarkson song blaring through the speakers.

Ten minutes later I am brought out of the car and walked into an unknown place. I'm trying to think where they could have taken me. Bowling? Karaoke? No, it's too quiet.

My blindfold is finally lifted, and I see that we are in a local dessert place, Chocoholic, which has great ice cream. Yum. I'm all for dessert right now.

Shortly after sitting down, the topic of college comes up.

"Brendan, when are you going to pick a freakin' school?" Reese asks me. "I want to know if I'm going to have you at Ohio State next year."

"I know. I have until May first, but I'll decide in the next couple weeks. It's giving me too much anxiety to wait any longer."

"But you've narrowed it down to OSU and Georgetown, right?" Kelly asks.

"Yep."

All of my friends have already chosen their destinations for next year. Reese and Kelly will be attending Ohio State, Natalie will be about an hour's drive from there at Ohio University, and Kara will be at Northwestern. Chris, of course, will be finishing his senior year of high school.

"All right, Brendan," Natalie says, "your favorite birthday memory. Go."

I take a few seconds to think about it. "I think you're looking at it."

"Stop," Natalie says.

"Seriously! I'm here with all of my closest friends, who took time to decorate my car today *and* plan a kidnapping."

"I feel like it's been hard for us all to get together this year," Reese says. "Unless it was someone's birthday or something, one of us always seemed to be busy."

Guilty. Once Mark and I started dating, I definitely became a lot less available.

"Well, it's going to get even harder once we go to college," Kelly says. "Then after that, it will be weddings that will bring us together, not birthdays."

"Dear God, I can't think about that," Kara says.

"Why not?" Chris says. "You're going to be first."

"No, no, no," she says.

"I'm going to be in your weddings, right?" I ask them.

"Yeah, you and Chris are going to be my best gays," Natalie says.

"Oh my gosh." I laugh. "Seriously, if I were to get married today, you would all be my bridesmaids, and Chris, my groomsman."

"I can't have a guy be in my wedding party," Kelly says.

"Why not?" Kara asks.

"Because the girls stand with the bride, the guys with the groom."

"That's not a rule," Kara says.

"It's your wedding," Reese says. "You can do whatever the hell you want."

"Not in the Catholic Church," Kelly says.

"What are they going to do?" Reese asks. "Stop the wedding?"

"It's just weird."

"If your best friend is a guy," I say, "why wouldn't you have him standing by your side on your most important day?"

"All right, all right, I get it," Kelly says. "Agree to disagree."

"That's just annoying," I continue. "It's not like I'd be close to your husband so I wouldn't be in *his* wedding party."

"Dude," she says.

"Sorry, I'm done now."

"Did I strike a nerve?"

"Apparently," I say, laughing.

"Well, I'm not going to get married so don't worry, Brendan," Natalie says.

"That's a lie," Kara says.

Toward the end of the night, Kelly pulls me aside. "I hope you're not mad about what I said earlier," she says. "It doesn't take away anything from our friendship."

"No, I know. I got upset because almost all my close friends are girls, and I wouldn't want to miss out on stuff just because I'm a guy. And my attitude is always, 'Who cares what people think? Do whatever you want.'"

"I understand. Let's be real—we're eighteen. This is ridiculous to even talk about. Who knows what will happen?"

"Good point."

Why *did* this strike such a nerve with me? I think that not having Mark has made me appreciate my friendships even more. Without them, I'd feel like I have nothing. So hearing Kelly say that she would never have me in her wedding made me question the bond that I have with her and my other girlfriends.

I know Natalie joked about Chris and me being her "best gays," but I would never want to be seen as an accessory. My bond with her and everyone else goes much deeper.

I feel pathetic for saying this, but by the time I get home that night, I'm bothered by the fact that Mark hasn't contacted me at all today. But it makes sense. I wouldn't wish *him* a happy birthday. It's yet another reminder that he and I are done.

A couple days later brings the opening night of *Anything Goes*. The excitement I get from a show opening is indescribable. Months of hard work pay off as you hear the applause and laughter from the crowd. Songs, dances, and scenes that have become monotonous during the last few weeks of rehearsal suddenly feel fresh now that an audience is watching.

At about six, I find myself in a familiar place—Chris's driveway. I'm playing chauffeur again, but I don't mind. Chris walks out of his house with a bag, presumably containing a change of clothes for the cast party tonight.

A few minutes after starting the drive to our school, I get a call from my sister, Sarah.

"Hello?" I answer.

"Brendan, hey."

"What's up?"

"Oh, nothing. Are you on the way to your show?"

"Yep."

"Are you excited?"

"Very."

"Good. I'm sure it will be great. Well, I don't really know how to say this, but Mom wanted me to call you because, you know, some of the aunts and uncles are coming to see your show tonight…"

"Yeah..."

"And she doesn't...well, after the show, she doesn't want you to...hug any of your guy friends."

What. The. Hell. I don't even say anything to her because I'm so pissed and confused. How is this conversation even happening right now?

"Okay?" she says after I stay silent.

"Okay," I say sternly. "Later." I hang up before she can say anything else.

Any excitement that I was feeling has disappeared. My stomach is now in knots for very different reasons.

"Everything okay?" Chris asks before I tell him what my sister said.

"What?" he exclaims. "Brendan, I'm sorry, no offense, but what is wrong with your mom? Who does that? Having your sister call you and—oh my gosh, my blood is boiling for you right now."

"Why does this have such an effect on me?" I ask. "I shouldn't be surprised. I was just so excited for tonight, and I know this is all I'll be able to think about now."

"I'm sorry, Brendan. Why didn't you talk back to your sister? Or better yet, why don't you call your mom and tell her how ridiculous she's being?"

"I don't know. I guess I find those conversations so uncomfortable I'd rather not have them. The awkwardness with my mom lasted for weeks after I told her I'm gay. I'd rather not even address it."

"Well, try to let it go, then. Think of how great the show is and how much people will love it."

"You're right. It bothers me because I know this is about something much bigger. Having my relatives see me hug a guy might make them think that I'm gay. God forbid."

"God forbid they see the real you."

"Did your parents do stuff like this after you came out?" I ask Chris.

"No," he quickly says. "They weren't happy about it, but they came around pretty quickly and supported me. I can't believe your mom would have your sister do that, knowing that you're so excited for tonight. Did she not think that would bring you down?"

"No, because she's thinking about herself right now. She doesn't want my relatives to question my sexuality, so she is going to make sure nothing tips them off tonight. She doesn't care if that upsets me."

"And since when does hugging a guy make you gay? It's so stupid."

"I know. Hugging girls certainly doesn't make me straight."

Chris and I continue to vent during our commute. Getting ready backstage for the show helps remove most of the lingering feelings I had regarding Sarah's phone call. I was not going to let this get me down the whole night. My mom wasn't okay with my being gay a couple months ago, and she's not okay with it today. Maybe that will change in the future; maybe it won't. I can't let it have such an effect on me.

The orchestra starts the overture at eight, and I hear the audience applaud. The energy stays high for the next two hours. The show goes great. Everyone's voice was in shape, the dances were in sync, and the jokes were perfectly delivered. The only mishap involved a set piece that fell mid-scene. At least the audience got a kick out of it.

After the show, I keep my hugging of boys to a minimum. I greet my mom and sister, but I don't say much more than hi to them. The telltale sign that I'm angry or upset is silence. I don't purposely do it, but I get so pissed off that I don't want to talk. My family received an extreme case of the silent treatment that night.

Chapter Seventeen

In my hands is my signed college acceptance letter. I have made a decision. At least I think I did. My fingers won't let me release the sealed envelope into the post office mailbox until I'm absolutely certain. I've spent countless hours debating this decision. I relax my fingers and watch the envelope disappear into the dark bin. I feel a sense of relief and excitement. Yes, this feels right. Next year I will be attending Ohio State.

Georgetown would be great and is in an amazing city, but I have the rest of my life to live in a big city like DC. I want to stay in Ohio for four more years and then will, no doubt, be ready for a big change when I graduate. Plus, my full academic scholarship to OSU was just too hard to pass up.

❖

With a group of friends as big as mine, we always seem to be celebrating someone's birthday. Tonight is Chris's, and he is having a low-key party at his house with his close friends. Yep, that includes Mark.

I knew it was going to happen eventually. After all, Chris knows nothing about my history with Mark, so he wouldn't think twice about inviting him. I'm actually surprised I was able to avoid a run-in with him for this long. But after almost two months, this Friday is the first time I will be seeing him in a non-school setting.

I thought about not showing up so I don't have to face him, but I'm actually feeling a lot better about the whole situation. It's a matter of months until I go off to college, and it would be a waste to spend that time moping around, reminiscing about our time together. I'd rather focus on creating some of the best memories with my closest friends, starting with tonight.

I'm not sure how it will go, but I'm going to make sure I look darn good. If Mark doesn't miss me right now, he will after seeing me. I like this revengeful yet somewhat pathetic side—Brendan with a little edge.

Fortunately, more people are at Chris's than I expected, so I'm able to mingle with everyone, making it easier to avoid Mark. He and I exchange hellos when he arrives, mainly because I don't want anyone to notice awkwardness between us, but it's not until later in the night when we have our first real interaction.

"Reese, get with Kelly," Chris says as he pulls out his camera. "Say 'Ohio State' on three."

"Wait," Reese says. "We need Brendan, too. Come on, B."

I give my corniest "Ohio State" while smiling for the camera.

"You're going to OSU?" Mark asks me after the picture is taken.

"Yep."

"That's awesome. When did you decide?"

"A couple weeks ago. Right at the deadline."

"I would have killed him if he didn't," Chris says. "Mark, you still up for taking road trips with me next year?"

"Sure," he says, looking at me to see my reaction. I give a polite smile.

"I don't know if I believe you, Mr. 'I Was Too Busy To See Your Show,'" Chris says to him.

"Yeah, what was up with that?" Natalie says.

"I'm sorry. I was planning to go Sunday but…"

"But…" Chris says.

Mark steals another glance at me before saying, "I was swamped with school work."

I know why he didn't go. He didn't want to have to stare at me for two hours. I can't blame him. Having to see him right now is somewhat torturous for me. I want nothing more than to talk to him like old times and spend the whole night laughing and flirting.

It's crazy how everything has changed. I guess it's the reality of breakups. Mark and I can no longer be close to each other because it's not healthy. Besides, no good would come from talking to him. The effect he has on me is strong, and I don't want to risk falling into him again.

I decide to exit the conversation before I get roped into talking to him. I head to the sink to get some water and lose myself in my thoughts.

"And how was that?" I hear from behind me.

"Gah!" I exclaim, turning to see Kara. "Where did you come from?"

"I was observing from a distance. You good?"

"I'm great."

She laughs. "That's convincing. How dare he talk to you?"

"I know, right?" We both subtly look across the room at him.

"Is he going to prom tomorrow?" Kara asks.

"Yep, he'll be there, because one sighting just isn't enough this weekend. At least it will be easier to avoid him at a five-hundred-person dance compared to tonight."

The next day, I pick up Reese at six-fifteen and head to Kelly's, where we are doing pictures. Her house is perfect for hosting, plus her mom loves it. Reese looks great in a red and white dress that she made. It's definitely unique and matches her quirky personality.

"Brendan, Reese, come on in," Kelly's mom says to us after opening the door.

"Hi, Mrs. Freeman," I say.

Kelly's mom is a character. It's neat how open she is with her kids. No topic is off-limits, including sex. She's also been so great to me and always manages to send me back home with leftovers, Christmas cookies, or any other food she can throw my way.

"Don't you guys look cute?" she says. "Reese, this is the dress you made?"

"Yep."

"Oh my gosh, it's beautiful. And Brendan, looking so handsome as usual."

"Thank you."

"I can't tell you how excited I am for the three of you to be together at school next year. I know you're going to make a bunch of new friends, but you'll realize how special your friendships are with each other. It's that Catholic bond, I'm telling you."

"Well, I've gone to school with Kelly for thirteen years," Reese says. "Thought I might as well make it seventeen."

"Isn't that wild?" Mrs. Freeman says. "Brendan, what are you studying next year? I don't even think I asked."

"Business, for now."

"Well, listen, you are smart enough to do anything, but let me tell you, I think the priesthood might be calling you."

"Dear God, Mom," Kelly says as she appears from her foyer. "Brendan, ignore her."

"You'd be great in business too," Mrs. Freeman reassures me. "But you have that spirit within you that would make a great priest. I'm just saying."

"Thank you," I say. "We'll see what happens."

After everyone gets to Kelly's, we go outside to pose in front of her picturesque garden. We do the typical "stand and smile" pictures, followed by the awkward school dance poses, and end with my favorite—model shots.

"Have fun, everyone," Kelly's mom says as we get ready to leave. "Remember, no drinking and no sex."

"Mom," Kelly says.

"I have a breathalyzer and am not afraid to use it." Gosh, I love her.

Arriving at the dance, we walk in to find the ballroom decorated with silver and navy streamers and a large sign that reads, "A Moment Like This."

"Wait, is that the theme?" I ask Reese, pointing to the sign.

"Yeah, I didn't tell you? Kelly Clarkson."

"Amazing. Tonight's got to be a good night with *that* theme."

"Yeah, last year was 'One Moment in Time.' They finally moved to the current century."

"Is it a requirement that the word 'moment' be in the theme?" I ask.

"Knowing our student council, probably."

We all enjoy a delicious dinner at our table. I want to scan the room to see who else I know at the dance, but I don't want to risk locking eyes with Mark. I maintain my tunnel vision as I continue to chat with everyone.

After dinner, my friends and I are among the first to go on the dance floor. It doesn't take long for me to spot a blue-eyed dirty blond about fifty feet away. I quickly turn away before he sees me. Operation Avoid Mark has officially begun. *Don't look*, I keep telling myself. Of course all I want to do is look.

I do my best to keep my focus on my friends. We keep dancing, taking turns going out to take our official prom pictures.

When Reese and I come back into the auditorium, I notice that Chris and Natalie are missing. I look across the room and see them talking to Mark. This is actually good. They are able to catch up with him and then rejoin our group, allowing me to bypass any interaction with him.

"You look so handsome tonight," Kelly says to me as Reese and I sit down at our table.

"Wow, thanks."

"Seriously, you clean up so nicely."

"If I had good fashion sense, I could look like this more often."

"No, I like your style," Reese says. "Casual hotness."

I laugh. "That's exactly what I'm going for. Kara, where's Andrew?"

"Talking to his friends over there."

"I take it you and Natalie are cool?" Kelly asks.

"Oh God, yeah. We fight, then act like nothing happened. But she's probably talking about me to Chris right now, saying how Andrew is abandoning me at my own dance."

"It's all good," I say. "That just means you can abandon him at Xavier's dance and hang out with us."

Toward the end of the night, I think that I'm in the clear from having to talk to Mark. Until, that is, I walk out of the bathroom and see him standing against the wall alone, staring at me. I'm caught so off guard that I stop in my tracks. Did he see me go to the bathroom and decide to wait outside for me?

He gives a slight smile before saying, "Hi, Brendan." I *hate* how good he looks.

"Hey, Mark. Having fun?"

He nods. "Did you get stage fright in there?" He's referencing my inability to go to the bathroom in public restrooms. I've always found the silence and close proximity so awkward. Often times, I am physically unable to go. I'm weird.

"I was good this time," I say. "The music was loud enough."

I feel my legs walk again, seemingly out of my control. I give him a smile before looking down and walking past him. I'm about to step foot into the ballroom but he stops me with his voice.

"Wait, Brendan." I pause for a second before turning to him, my heartbeat reacting as it always does with Mark. "How have you been? I didn't really get a chance to talk to you last night."

"Good. Busy."

"How's tennis going?"

"It's good. Our team is pretty solid this year."

"And I'm sure you're undefeated this season," he says, smiling.

"Of course." I try to smile back but don't feel like faking it. "How's everything with you?" I don't really want to hear how his life has been, but I ask to be polite.

"Pretty good. Soccer's done, so I've had more free time."

"Nice. Well, I'm going to head back in." I lean toward the door, but I can tell he wants to say something.

"Brendan…it's good to see you."

My face remains expressionless.

"And I know this is unfair for me to say," he continues, "but I miss hanging out with you."

I let out a sigh of anger and look down.

"I know," he says. "I'm sorry."

"Come on, Mark," I say, looking back up at him. "What am I supposed to do with that? You're right. It *is* unfair for you to say that. *You* chose how this turned out. Look, I don't hold any resentment toward you, but you've got to understand that it doesn't help when…" I trail off as I try to organize my thoughts.

"I'm sorry," he says. "It's just…last night at Chris's, it was so weird not talking to you. It's like we're strangers."

"Well, that's what happens after two people—"

"There you are," I hear from behind me. I turn to see Reese at the entranceway of the ballroom. "I thought I lost my date."

I do my best to snap out of my anger so that she doesn't notice. "Hey, Reese. Sorry. I'm ready. See you, Mark," I say to him before rejoining the group.

I'm thankful that she interrupted our conversation. I don't want to know what else Mark would have said to me.

Although the dance is almost over, I've still got a long night ahead of me. After prom comes After-Prom. I'd much rather go straight home to be alone with my thoughts, but I guess it's better to have some more distractions for the night.

After the dance finishes up, the crew and I make a pit stop at Kelly's to change clothes before heading to Dave and Buster's for the After-Prom celebration. The whole place is rented out for us, and it actually looks like a lot of fun.

I start off at the mini basketball game, where I maintain a long winning streak before being knocked out by a fellow classmate. Next, I catch up with some friends outside of my prom group and play skee ball.

As I'm playing, I hear the most terrible singer belting out some
'90s song. After scanning the room, I find the source of the wretched
sound: karaoke. I immediately head that direction to find a couple of
my theater friends going through the songbook.

"Hey guys," I say to them.

"What's up, Brendan?" Beth says. "Should Dave and I do
Christina Aguilera or Stacie Orrico?"

"You're forgetting about our favorite singer." Beth and I share
the same obsession with Kelly Clarkson. We both saw her in concert
last year with a couple others.

"*You* do Kelly!" she says.

"I was going to anyway." I laugh.

Apparently karaoke isn't too popular tonight because after Beth
and Dave belt out their Christina song, it's my turn.

"Since U Been Gone" is my go-to karaoke track, but it's never
felt more appropriate than it does tonight. As I'm singing, I see
Reese and Kara join the small crowd of spectators. Kara shakes her
head while smiling at me. I give her a wink.

As I finish the last line, my friends erupt in applause. Man,
I feel good. All I needed was a three-minute therapy session with
Kelly to turn my attitude around.

After singing, I bounce around to a few more games, collecting
an obscene number of tickets, which I use to buy a squirt gun and
stuffed animal. I'll never use either.

A little later, Reese and I say our good-byes before getting
into my car. We start to talk about the night, sharing some funny
moments, but after a pause, she asks, "Are you okay?"

"Um, yeah."

She's not convinced. "Brendan, it's easy to tell when
something's bothering you. You become super quiet. You seem fine
now, but something was up at the dance. I'm not trying to pry, but
I'm here if you want to talk." I don't say anything. "And I think I
know what it's about," she adds.

"What?" I ask, intrigued.

"Mark."

I look over at her. "Mark what?" I'm more curious than anything.

"Well, that's a good question." She laughs. "But on my birthday, when Natalie and Chris were grilling you about him, I could tell you were hiding something. And then walking into your conversation with him tonight, it felt very tense." I nod but don't say anything.

"Are you guys dating...or...?"

"No...but we did."

"Say what? For how long?"

"A couple months. It started right after New Year's."

Reese continues to drill me. Why couldn't you tell anyone? Why did you break up? What did you talk about with him tonight? I give her all the details.

"So no one else knows about you two?" she asks.

"Well..." I say before laughing.

"If you even say 'Kara'..."

"You can't get mad at me. I'm sad and depressed, remember?"

"All right, that's it," she says, pretending to sound fed up.

"I begged Mark to let me tell her. And she knew the most about the situation so she would have been the hardest to fool," I explain as I pull into Reese's driveway.

"Well listen, talk to me if you need to vent, or scream, or get milkshakes or whatever."

I laugh. "Milkshakes always do the trick."

"But seriously, are you okay? I'm sure tonight wasn't easy."

"I'm okay. Honestly. Tonight just rattled me a little bit."

"Well, keep me posted on the whole situation."

I nod. "Thanks for taking me tonight. I had a lot of fun."

Chapter Eighteen

About a week and a half after the dance, I'm shocked when I receive a text from Mark, asking me if we can meet up to talk. I immediately get nervous as I try to think of the reason he wants to get together. I'm guessing he wants to apologize for how everything went down with us and may even ask if we can be friends.

I don't know if I can go through with it. Talking to him for two minutes at prom was enough to make me go crazy for a little while. If it's a continuation of our conversation that night, I may not want to know what he has to say.

I don't respond for a few hours, but ultimately I agree to meet him. I appreciate his directness, and although hearing what he has to say might be tough, I'd rather know for sure what's on his mind as opposed to going crazy trying to figure it out on my own.

Later that evening, he and I meet to get some ice cream, an activity that can be very quick if need be. We start with small talk as we wait in line, but by the time we sit down at an outside table, it's time to get to business.

"First off, thank you for meeting with me," he says.

"No problem."

"I don't want to waste your time, so I'll jump into it. I've been trying to figure out how I'm even going to start this, but first I want to tell you that I'm sorry. I'm sorry for hurting you and for not being strong enough to keep going with our relationship. And I'm sorry for waiting this long to talk to you. You put up with a lot of crap—

hiding it from your friends even though they know you're gay and would be happy for you, hiding it from your mom. I'm—"

"Well, my mom wasn't your fault. I would have hidden it from her no matter who I was dating."

"I know, but I'm sure it was hard for you to juggle all of it, especially knowing that I was so paranoid toward the end."

I nod to agree with him. "It's okay. I appreciate the apology."

"You don't how much I wish I could just live my life and not care about what everyone thinks about me. And I've tried to convince myself these past few weeks, but I don't know."

"It's okay. We don't need to rehash everything." The more he talks, the sadder I get. I've spent the last couple months trying to bury my feelings. I don't want to dig them up.

"I know, but wait. I have to tell you the other day, I was thinking about the night Eva saw us."

"Oh, hell," I say, giving up. He clearly needs to get this stuff off his chest. "Fond memories. Continue."

He laughs. "But I wasn't thinking about the moment she saw us. I was thinking about the moments before that, when we were talking and kissing in my basement. And I was thinking about how happy I was in those moments.

"When Eva caught us, I thought my world was going to come crashing down. But it didn't. She never told my parents and my life went on. If I had known at that moment that everything was going to be okay, I wouldn't have let you go. At the time, I felt I had no other choice. What I've realized since then is that I really want you back in my life. And I asked you to meet me today to see if there's any way you'd consider taking me back."

I stare at him expressionless, trying to comprehend what he's asking me.

"Because, Brendan," he continues, "these past few weeks, I have missed you *so* much. I guarantee you that I've missed you more than you've missed me. And it's ridiculous because *I'm* the one who's preventing myself from being happy, just like you told me.

"That's because I'm battling between the desire to be with you and the fear that people will find out. That fear is still there and very strong, but what I've realized these last couple weeks is that my desire to be with you is much stronger. So I could remove you from my life along with the fear of anyone finding out about us, or I could keep you in my life and deal with the obstacles when they arise."

"Wow," I say.

"That's what you said after I told you I liked you in January."

"I don't know what's caught me more off guard—that moment or this one."

His outpouring overwhelms me. I was honestly not expecting this. I don't even know where to begin.

"Okay, first off," I start, "I appreciate the honesty, and I accept your apology. And I don't want you to feel bad about it. I knew what I was getting into when we started dating, and I understood that our relationship was going to be a secret from everyone.

"And if you're going to be honest, I might as well too," I continue. "The past couple months have been rough. Time has helped, but I still feel a void I didn't have before I met you. But, Mark, why couldn't you have told me this a month ago? Or better yet, *two* months ago?"

"I know. I wish it hadn't taken me this long to come to this realization."

"I have very mixed feelings right now. A part of me is thrilled, but I wish you had said, 'I want to be with you *and* I don't care who knows.' If we were to date again, how would it be different? What if people find out about us? Heck, Reese already figured us out."

"What? How?"

"Walking in our conversation at prom was the final piece of the puzzle for her."

"Okay, yeah, that was my fault," he says. "As for the possibility of other people figuring it out, I've thought about this a lot. Honestly, Brendan, it would depend on the circumstance. With Eva, there was nothing I could do; she caught us red-handed. With Reese, I don't really mind. She's not going to go around telling people. But let's say someone at school were to find out and ask me about it. I'd probably deny it and laugh it off."

"And then would you start freaking out and end things with me again? I just want us to both be realistic about this. The same elements would be working against us."

"I totally understand," he says. "But I see it as…it's a matter of days until we're done with school. Then it's summer break, which will give us so much more freedom to hang out. You won't have to lie to your friends every weekend about why you're busy because you and I could see each other any night of the week. And then you leave for college, so it would be much harder for people to figure things out then."

"That's true," I say. "Although it adds a new complication of long distance." I look down to gather my thoughts.

"What are you thinking?"

"I'm thinking that I need to think about this."

"Absolutely. Look, I came here tonight with no expectations. Do you need any more information from me to help you decide?"

I laugh. "I don't think so. I want to sort out my thoughts."

"Well, can I say one more thing while I have the chance?" he asks. "Whatever you decide, I want you to know how thankful I am that you came into my life. I can't say enough good things about you, and I will always want only the best for you. You're a really special guy."

"Are you trying to sway my decision?"

"No!" He laughs. "I just don't know if I'll have another opportunity to tell you how I feel."

Our conversation is over, but we've barely started eating our ice cream. I'm not sure what to do. After a few seconds of silence, I say, "All right, I'm going to head home."

"Don't go yet," he quickly says. "We just sat down."

"I know, but we talked about what we needed to talk about."

"At least finish your ice cream. It's dangerous to eat while you're driving." I crack a slight smile. "Five minutes. That's all I'm asking for. Let's just sit and talk. No complications, no guards up. Just two people catching up."

"Okay," I finally agree. "Two months is a lot to catch up on in five minutes."

"Let's start with tennis. What's the latest?"

"I won Sectionals. Districts are in two days."

"When are States?"

"Next Friday and Saturday if I qualify." Mark gives me a glare. "I've got to say that to try to appear humble."

"It's *me* you're talking to," he says. "You'll win Districts, right? Be honest."

"I've got it in the bag. And then the State tournament is at Ohio State, so it will be cool to get a preview of where I'll be living in a few months. I've been there before, but I'll have a different perspective now."

"That's sweet. I've actually never seen the campus. Are you going to explore a little bit?"

"Yeah, definitely. All right, so what's new with you?" I ask.

"Well, I'm more than ready for summer. I have a countdown going in my assignment notebook."

"Any big summer plans?"

"Actually, I'm going to Italy with my family in July. We're going to travel to a few other countries when we're there too."

"That's sweet."

The more Mark and I talk, the more I feel my guard coming down. After a little while, I look at my watch and realize that twenty minutes have gone by, well past the five minutes to which I agreed.

"Is my time up?" he asks, knowing the answer. I nod. He and I get up and walk to the parking lot.

"Thanks for meeting with me," he says. "Seriously. Good luck at Districts. And if I don't talk to you before States, good luck with that too. I wish I could see you play."

"Hey, I'm always happy to have a crowd."

"Are your friends going?"

"I don't think so. Reese mentioned it, but I doubt she'll go. All right, Mark, have a good night."

"You too. A hug for old time's sake?" he asks, his arms extended.

I stare at him, shaking my head, but reach out my arms and give him a quick hug.

As soon as I get into my car to go home, I call Kara. When faced with a decision that I don't want to make, I turn to friends and have them decide for me. At least I gather their opinions before deciding. The decision as to whether to take Mark back is no different.

"Hello?" Kara answers.

"Emergency. I need your advice."

"Okay," she laughs.

"I just got ice cream with Mark, and he said that he wants me back. I don't know what to do."

"As if *I* do?"

"Yes. You know me better than I know myself."

"Okay, first tell me your reaction to this."

"It's interesting. Part of me is thrilled because I've missed him so much, and I had so much fun with him when we were together. Even talking to him tonight was so nice. Then part of me is thinking that nothing will change, so it's not going to end well. He still would want to keep it a secret from everyone."

"Well, what prompted him to do this? Didn't he decide that dating you isn't worth the risk of people finding out?"

"He now says that being with me is worth that risk. He likes me too much."

"Hmm."

"What?" I ask.

"I don't know how long you would be able to pull off the whole secret relationship thing. His sister already caught you guys. What happens when his friends or his parents do? He'll freak out even more."

"Get out of my brain, Kara. Those are my thoughts exactly."

"And think about a few months from now when you'll be at Ohio State. You'll have plenty of guys to choose from. Is your connection with Mark so strong that you want to prevent yourself from seeing what else is out there when you move to Columbus? Obviously, follow your gut. I'm just trying to see the big picture." After a pause, she adds, "I mean, let's be honest. You never listen to my advice anyway."

"That's not true."

"Which way are you leaning on this one?"

"I'm honestly fifty fifty. The sadness I felt when he and I broke up was awful. I don't know if I want to risk going through that again."

"Well, you could look at it this way…if you two date again, and he panics and breaks up with you, you'll absolutely be done for good and will be able to officially move on."

"So, now you're telling me I *should* take him back?"

"I'm not responsible for this decision. This is all on you. I'm just thinking out loud."

"Well, hey, you and Andrew broke up once and you two are good now."

"True," she says hesitantly. "But our reason for breaking up wasn't the fear that someone would find out about us."

I laugh. "All right, thanks for your advice as usual."

"Brendan, take time to think about this. There's no rush. Mark certainly took *his* time."

She's right. Mark needs to know what it's like to sweat a little bit. I had to wait a couple months to hear him say he wants to date me again. He can stand to wait a week or so as to whether I feel the same way. Besides, I have bigger things coming up on which I need to focus. Next week is packed with final exams, the state tennis tournament, and graduation.

CHAPTER NINETEEN

While deliberating over the next week, I realize that it has become a battle between my heart, which is telling me to date Mark again, and my brain, which is telling me to not even go down that path.

Fortunately, my deliberation didn't take my focus off the district tennis tournament. The kid I played in the finals put up a good fight, but other than that, I breezed through all of my matches.

Today brought my final final exam of my high school career. As I was driving home from my last day on campus, I looked back on the last four years. A part of me feels like they've flown by, but at the same time, each year has a distinct place in my memory.

I see freshman year as sort of a continuation of eighth grade. My friends and I were still without driver's licenses, and we didn't really branch out that much when it came to meeting people. For some reason, I remember hanging out in Reese's basement a lot on the weekends, watching MTV.

I also remember not having that much confidence. Or rather, I remember being worried about what people thought of me. I think that going to an all-guys school made me feel like no one understood who I was. In grade school, I had all of my close friends with me; at Xavier, I wasn't close to anyone.

Sophomore year definitely brought an upswing, at least in my social life. I did the school musical at St. Mary's, which had the best cast that I've ever worked with. I had so much fun and laughed nonstop. School itself, however, was hard. AP US History was almost the death of me, thanks to my teacher.

And then there's junior year. Probably the most significant year of my life. Not just because I came to terms with my sexuality, which was definitely important. I also felt like I transitioned from young, naïve teen to mature almost adult. My friends and I faced more serious life events, and as a result, our friendships grew. I also think that I became more confident in who I was and how I felt.

As for senior year, I can't help but smile when I think about it. It had its ups and downs, but as a whole, it was the most exciting time of my life. It was also probably the most fun. And this Sunday, when I graduate, it will all come to an end.

The next night I drive down to Columbus with my mom for the state tennis tournament. The top sixteen players from across the state are brought to this tournament. Our doubles team had a good shot, but they lost in the qualifying round of Districts, so I'm the only one here from my school. Two matches will be played on the first day and two on the second day for those who make it that far.

Fortunately, when I wake up the next morning, I'm not too nervous. I have a very competitive spirit. I want to win and will try my hardest to do it, but I'm not going to be hard on myself if I don't.

My first day is a success. I made it to the semifinals last year, so I'm happy to have at least made it that far again this year. I don't want to take a step back. That'd be embarrassing.

My semifinal match starts at nine-thirty on the morning of day two. The kid I'm playing is a junior from a school in Cincinnati. During our warm-up, I can tell it's going to be a tough match. He hits the ball hard. Though with that amount of pace, I'm sure he makes a good amount of errors.

It takes me a few games to get used to his style of playing.

I'm the one who usually whips my forehand across the net to make winners. With him, I'm having trouble getting control of the points. After only twenty minutes, I'm down 4–1. I like to exert as little effort as possible with each point to save energy, but he has other plans for me. He keeps running me around all over the court. Now I'm getting pissed. I take my anger out on the ball and finally start to get into my groove.

Unfortunately, it's too late to salvage the set. I lose it 6–4. It's all right. I've picked up some momentum that hopefully will carry into the next set.

I start the second set strong, but he stays right with me. We continue to stay neck and neck until it is 5–5. I win the next game to take the lead 6–5. Okay, Brendan. One more game. Just win. If I get to a third set, I know I can pull this off.

My coach gives me some reassurance at the changeover and tells me to relax and just get the ball in. I don't play the game as conservatively as he'd like, but I still manage to win the game and set.

"You're trying to give me a heart attack, aren't you?" he asks me before I start the third and final set.

"I know. I'm sorry. I'm low on energy. I had to go for winners."

"All right, well just take your time between each point to catch your breath. Don't rush."

"Got it."

The third set is the quickest of the three. 6–2. Thankfully, I end up on top. My opponent's the one who ran out of steam halfway through. Once I got the 4–2 lead, I knew I had it in the bag.

"You're going to the state finals," my coach tells me, grabbing my shoulder as I walk off the court.

I turn in the tennis balls to the official, and then head to my mom, where I'm greeted with a hug and smile. I tried to avoid looking up at her during the match because I knew she'd be a nervous wreck. Is it bad that everyone around me gets more nervous than I do? I promise I care. I just want to have fun while I play too.

My mom and I head to a restaurant close by to get a quick bite to eat. I keep my lunch light but drink about a gallon of water to stay hydrated. My final match doesn't start until two, so I have time to relax when I get back to the courts.

After sitting on the bleachers for a while, I decide to get my legs moving a little bit. I pace back and forth across the parking lot, listening to music. I think I hear someone say my name so I take one of my earphones out and look up toward the tennis courts. Nothing.

"B!" I hear again, realizing that it's coming from behind me. I turn around to see Reese and Mark walking toward me.

"What?" I scream before walking toward them. "I cannot believe this."

"How's it going?" Reese says. "Please tell us you made the finals. Or are you playing for third place?"

"Finals. But wait, I need a moment to take this all in. You two drove here together?"

Mark is visibly nervous as he says, "I really wanted to see you play, so I texted Reese to see if she'd be up for it."

"And I responded, 'Who is this?'" Reese says.

I laugh. "Mark has a way of getting people's numbers."

"I really hope I'm not overstepping my bounds," Mark says. "Last week, when I mentioned that I'd like to see you play, you didn't seem to completely reject that idea. Then I asked Reese if she thought you'd be mad."

"I told him you love an audience, so you'll be thrilled," Reese says.

"You know me so well. You're fine, Mark. No worries. I'm glad you guys are here. I have so much more energy now.

"How was the car ride?" I ask. "I can only imagine how fun it was."

"It involved a lot of Britney Spears music," Mark says unenthusiastically.

"Oh, so Reese showed you how good a singer she was?"

"And dancer," Reese adds.

The three of us chat a little more before heading back to the tennis courts. About twenty minutes before my match time, I go to sit near my mom and coach. I don't want them to think my friends are distracting me from my focus.

It's finally time. As I walk onto the court, my nerves kick in. So many people are watching us, including a couple of journalists holding their cameras. Of all the matches in high school tennis, this is the big one. My opponent notices me staring out at everyone.

"Big crowd, huh?" he says.

"Seriously. The pressure's on."

We put our bags down and pull out our racquets. "Good luck," he says with a smile before we walk to opposite ends of the court. Gosh, he's making it hard for me to get my game face on. If it were anyone else, I would think that he's being disingenuous, but this kid is so nice. Well, at least if I lose, I'll be happy for him.

About forty minutes into the match, I find myself in a similar position as this morning. I lose the first set 6–2. Why do I always take a while to get warmed up? My coach gives me a pep talk to reassure me that I'm not out yet.

"Remember this morning?" he says. "You proved to yourself that you are able to come back. Just forget about this set. It's zero zero again." I nod.

I've found myself in this situation a countless number of times throughout my tennis career. When I was twelve, I was once down 6–0, 5–0 and came back to win the match. Apparently I play better under pressure.

I start the second set strong and take the lead 3–1. My fan club in the stands pushes me to take the set 6–3.

Going into the third set, my coach tells me to keep doing what I'm doing. Of course I know that my opponent will mix things up with his play in the third set to mess up my momentum, just like I did with him in the second set.

After an exhausting twelve games, I find myself tied with him 6–6. Time for a third set tiebreaker. Seriously? Tiebreakers are the only time I get nervous while playing because every point is so important. The first one to seven points wins as long as he wins by two points.

The key with tiebreakers is to take an early lead. Unfortunately, that doesn't happen. A few minutes after starting, I find myself tied 4–4 with him. After two more points, he's up 6–4. He now has two match points.

I hit a strong serve to start the next point, which gives me control. After a rally back and forth, he hits a ball short, which allows me to approach the net and go for a winner. I whip my forehand down the line, but it doesn't make it across the net. Crap. It's done. I see the ball roll back toward me while the crowd erupts in cheers—well, most of the crowd. I look up to see my opponent approach the net.

"Good match," he says, extending his hand.

"You too," I say, shaking it with mine. "Congratulations."

"Thanks."

As I step off the court, my coach gives me a handshake. "Hey, runner-up at States. That's a huge accomplishment. You should be proud of yourself."

After greeting my mom, I'm bombarded by a bunch of other people I don't know who tell me how good a match it was, and that I did a great job. I finally make my way to Reese and Mark, who aren't quite sure how to comfort me.

"Good try, Brendan," Reese tells me. "I'm sorry."

"You played great," Mark adds. "There's nothing more you could have done."

"Thanks, guys. It's all good. He played awesome."

"Hey, you at least improved from last year," Mark adds. "From third place to second."

"A bronze and a silver," I say. "I'm Michelle Kwan at the Olympics."

As they try to distract me some more, someone from some Cincinnati newspaper asks me if he can ask me a few questions.

"Look at that. Even the loser gets some fame," I whisper to Reese and Mark before stepping aside with the reporter.

❖

The very next night, I have my graduation ceremony. You know how people aren't supposed to cheer for the graduating seniors when their names are called? Yeah, my friends don't listen to those rules.

"Brendan Madden," my principal says before I walk forward to get my diploma.

"Brendan!" I then hear from the balcony. "Go, B! Woohoo!" Fortunately, they're not too obnoxious.

As I sit back down in my seat, I think about all of the people sitting with me right now, some I've never spoken to and others with whom I've shared a seemingly endless number of hours.

I will never see some of these people again in my life. We will all go our separate ways, and although I'll no doubt cross some of their paths, others will now forever be in the past. It's strange.

After the ceremony, I take pictures with my family before meeting my friends, who congratulate me and tell me how boring the ceremony was. Among them is Mark, who came with Chris tonight.

"The kid who gave the speech," Natalie says.

"Terrible?" I ask.

"Yes. How is he your valedictorian?"

"He's brilliant but apparently unable to write something with substance."

"Yeah, it was pretty generic," Reese says. "I want to get his number, though. The key is to marry a cute nerd. He'll be rich and successful, *and* he won't leave you."

As my friends argue what qualities make a good husband, I quietly ask Mark if he is able to talk tonight. He's caught a little off guard, but he says yes.

Separately, we head to a coffee shop and have a little chitchat at first.

"Can I just say that I swear I'm not stalking you?" Mark says. "I told Chris weeks ago that I would go to the graduation ceremony with him."

"Sure you did," I say jokingly.

"How does it feel to graduate?"

"Crazy. I'm excited, though. I'm ready to get some independence and have a change of city."

"I think you'll have the best of both worlds. You'll be in a fun city with so many new people, but it's not too far away from your friends and family. A visit home will be easy."

"Yeah, exactly. So," I say, shifting the mood of the conversation.

"Here we go," Mark says.

"So, I'll make this quick. I've made you wait long enough. I've been thinking things through, and although I still have feelings for you, dating you again would have all of the original complications and obstacles. It's definitely not an ideal scenario and the odds are stacked against us.

"However," I continue, "I know myself well enough to know that there's no way I could leave this coffee shop without taking you back." A big smile forms on his face. "I got so excited seeing you at my tennis match yesterday. I like you too much and would always wonder what could have happened if I didn't try this again with you. But listen. Know that I'm going to be cautious."

"Understood. I will be better than before. I promise you that."

"That's not saying much. Kidding."

"Thank you for giving this another chance. Come here." He stands up with his arms wide to give me a hug.

"In public? Whoa, maybe things *will* be better."

I embrace him. It feels so good to hold him in my arms again. I have concerns, but I'm willing to risk getting hurt again in order to be with him.

"I asked you to meet me in person today, so you knew it had to be *good* news, right?" I ask.

"That's what I was hoping, but I also thought that karma would have you reject me to my face."

For months I've been wondering what Mark told Eva the night she caught us. He tells me that after I left, he went to her room and convinced her to talk about it. He was pretty honest with her. He told her that he and I started dating recently, that I'm the first guy he's liked, and that he doesn't know if he's gay. She was very understanding and agreed not to tell their parents.

"She also said that she loves you, so she supports it," Mark tells me.

"Aw. Does that mean you're going to tell her that we're dating again?"

"Um…I don't think so." I can tell he's scared to see my reaction.

"I was half kidding. I figured."

"You can tell Reese and Kara."

"I might want to keep it to myself for now. See how it goes at first."

"Oh no. Little confidence."

"Just cautious, like I said."

CHAPTER TWENTY

The first time Mark and I hung out post-reconciliation was kind of a transition, more like friends catching up. I definitely had my guard up. I wanted to make sure he wasn't going to change his mind about how he felt. Fortunately, his actions have shown that he takes this seriously.

I told Mark I might want to keep our relationship to myself, but that lasted about forty-eight hours. To make up for my past favoritism, I actually told Reese first, followed by Kara, both of whom weren't the least bit surprised.

I feel like I'm asking for trouble by keeping my other friends in the dark. Whether it's months from now or years from now, they're going to find out about Mark and me. And it's not going to be pretty once they learn that Kara and Reese knew the whole time. Maybe I can keep that fact from them. I'm not going to worry about that now. I'd rather have a couple of friends who know, regardless of how pissed off people might get in the future. It's two less people that I have to try to fool.

When Mark and I got back together, he said that he would be better this time—less paranoid, less of a flight risk. Little did I know that a couple of weeks into summer, we would run into someone who would test just how much Mark meant what he said.

After talking about it for months, Mark and I finally get around to playing tennis against each other at our local recreation center. It has a bunch of outdoor courts I like to take advantage of in the summer. It's the first time I'm playing since losing the state title. I figured why not find the worst player I know? Crushing him will make me feel better.

"You know you have to bring your game *way* down, right?" Mark says as we step onto the court.

"On one condition. You play shirtless." He gives me a look to indicate he's not pleased with my request. "Oh, come on. No one likes a farmer's tan. And I want eye candy while I'm running you around."

"I want eye candy too."

"Fine," I say, taking my shirt off.

"Yay," he says, taking his off as well.

Shortly after we start playing, I realize I have to bring my game down much farther than I anticipated. We're talking like thirty percent of my usual pace. It cracks me up to see someone so athletic be so uncoordinated at playing tennis.

"This is pathetic," he says after we play a few games.

"No," I say unconvincingly.

"Have you ever played someone this bad?"

"God, yes."

"Like in a real match, I mean."

"Yes. Actually, there was one match at sectionals last year where I had to play a girl. She wore jeans."

"No."

"Yeah. During our warm-up, I could tell that she was terrible."

"Why wasn't she in the girls' division?"

"I don't know. I know like five years ago some girl got to play in the boys' division because she was just too good for the girls'. She ended up getting third or fourth place at States."

"Damn."

"For the girl I played, that was not the case. But anyway, after like four games, I realized that I hadn't lost a point yet. I was playing nice and easy against her, kind of like how I'm playing with you."

Mark laughs. "Great."

"So then I start to think to myself, 'Oh my gosh, Brendan. You could go this whole match without losing a single point. That would be amazing.' That's forty-eight points in a row. So by the time I'm up 6–0, 5–0, I'm shaking because I don't want to hit it out or in the net."

"Please tell me you let this girl win a point."

"No. Isn't that awful? That's so unlike me, right? You'd think I would feel bad for her."

"That's awful but also hilarious."

"Yeah, so don't feel too bad. You've already won a couple points today."

"Right. I really earned those," he says sarcastically. "Okay, I want you to go all out during this next game. Seriously. I want to see what it's really like to play you."

"All right, if you're sure."

As Mark and I are talking, two guys walk onto the court next to us.

"Mark!" one of them says. "What's going on, man?"

"Hey, Ted," Mark says, caught off guard.

Ted looks over at me. "Hey," he says as I try to figure out if I know him. His face looks vaguely familiar.

Mark interjects, trying to get hold of the conversation. "Ted, this is my friend, Brendan." *Boyfriend*, I think, but never dare say.

"Yeah, I know you," Ted says. "Aren't you friends with Chris McNeill?"

"Yeah. How do you know Chris?" Who is this guy?

"He dated my cousin."

"Who's your cousin?"

"Alex Stanton."

"Oh, wow. Okay, I know him." Chris and Alex dated for about six months, a long time when you're sixteen. "How do you guys know each other?" I ask, referencing Ted and Mark. I look over at Mark to gauge his reaction. He's keeping his poker face on, but I'm sure he's not too fond of this interaction right now.

"We've played soccer together forever," Mark says.

"Yeah, this kid and I go way back," Ted says, grabbing Mark's shoulder.

"But you don't go to Xavier," I say to Ted.

"No. How do you two know each other? You're a year older than us, right?" What the heck? I've never even heard of this guy, and he knows all about me.

"I am. How did you know that? Who are you?"

He laughs. "I've been stalking you for years. No, I think I hung out with you last year with Alex and Chris, but we weren't introduced. It was a big group. I think we went bowling?"

"Okay, that sounds right."

"I also saw you in the Xavier musical this past spring," Ted says.

"Oh. Did you like it?" I ask, suddenly getting excited now that the topic of conversation revolves around me.

"Yeah, it was great. *You* were great."

"Thanks. Anyway, to answer your question, Mark and I met through Chris, pretty much."

Ted nods. "Well, I'll let you get back to playing. Look at you guys and your glistening bodies. Trying to give people a show?"

"Yeah, is it working?" I ask.

Ted laughs. "Working for me. See you, guys."

Mark gives a slight laugh while Ted heads back to his court. After another thirty minutes of running around, Mark and I end the athletic portion of our day. We say bye to Ted and head to my car.

"Why…" Mark says to me after walking off the court. "*Why* did we have to be shirtless?"

I laugh. "It's hot and we wanted a tan. Come on, that's normal. So give me the scoop. Are you close to him? Are you freaking out right now?"

"No, I'm fine. I swear. But yeah, we're pretty close when it comes to my soccer friends."

"Well, he was really nice. And he seems very gay-friendly. Maybe a little *too* gay-friendly."

"Oh my gosh, you think everyone's gay."

I laugh. "Okay, true, but come on. He loved that we were half naked, and he was super nice."

"Well, if he *is* gay, you're taken so he can back off."

"Whoa, is someone jealous?" I ask.

"You guys were flirting a little bit too much."

"Aw, don't worry. I'm yours. Did you have any idea his cousin dated Chris?"

"None. What the hell was that? This world is too small."

"Well, I'm happy that you're not freaking out," I say.

"I mean, it's not like he saw us making out or something. But as you said, he seems very gay-friendly, so even if he had…"

"Even if he had…?"

"He would be cool with it."

"Yeah, he'd probably ask if we want a third." Mark shakes his head in embarrassment. "But would *you* have been cool with it?" I ask.

"Well, I'd rather have *him* find out than other people on my team."

I can't believe what I'm hearing. Mark is actually imagining what it would be like if someone in his life knew about us? It's a big step. I don't poke any further because I don't want to make a big deal about it, but I'm definitely taking note of this conversation.

A few minutes later, I pull into Mark's driveway to drop him off.

"Want to hang out for a little bit?" he asks.

"Sure. Is anyone home?" Since getting back together, I've only been inside his house twice. Both times it was empty.

"I don't think so. My parents' car isn't here."

After walking inside, I immediately see Eva in the kitchen. Oh boy.

"Hi, Eva."

"Hey, Brendan. How are you?"

"I'm good. It's been a while." *The last time I saw you, I was on top of your brother*, I think. "Are you having a good summer?"

"Yes, it's so nice to have a break from school. And I just got my license."

"Congrats."

I turn to Mark, expecting to see a worried look on his face, but instead, he is smiling.

"What?" I say to him.

He gives a slight laugh. "Eva knows."

I turn to look at her. She gives me a smile and nod.

"Since when?"

"I told her this week," Mark says. "I wouldn't have been able to hide it from her all summer with you coming over here."

"I'm no fool," she says.

"Oh my gosh. I love that you didn't tell me, Mark."

"Seeing your face just now was too classic," he says.

I was always worried about my first interaction with Eva, especially since I'd have to pretend like Mark and I are just friends now. I didn't see how she was going to be convinced. Thankfully, I don't have to worry about that anymore. This will make this summer much easier.

Beyond that, I'm thrilled that Mark is okay with Eva knowing about us. It gives me hope that someday he won't care if other people in his life know as well.

CHAPTER TWENTY-ONE

I can't believe how fast this summer has been flying by. It's now only a matter of weeks until I move to Columbus. I've been staying busy hanging out with Mark and my friends, getting everything organized for college, and giving tennis lessons to kids.

It's actually kind of cool how my tennis job came about. This girl I know asked me if I wanted to organize a summer program at these outdoor courts in a development close to where I live. We made flyers and solicited people we know. We got a great turnout, and although we don't charge much, we've made pretty good money.

Another activity taking up my time is graduation parties. I've been going to them literally every weekend. Tonight is finally my own.

Most people have one party, which includes both their friends and family. I couldn't imagine my friends and family intermingling, so I decided to have two separate ones. The family one was last weekend. Tonight is friends only. Well, friends plus boyfriend. It's funny but also sad that Mark has never stepped foot inside my house. That will change tonight.

Kara is the first one to arrive. "I have a present for you," she says after walking in with a gift bag.

"No. We all agreed no presents."

"It's stupid, don't worry."

I look inside to find a card and a box of Pop-Ice freezer pops. "So random. Thanks."

"Those should last you the rest of summer."

Reese arrives about ten minutes later, followed by Mark.

"Hey, buddy," I say to him after opening the front door.

"Hello," he says before giving me a wink in lieu of a hug. My dogs run up to him, eager to say hello. "Agh, I finally get to meet these two." He scoops up the poodle, Pepper, who seems exceptionally affectionate toward him.

"Aren't they cute?"

We head toward the kitchen, where everyone else is gathered. Reese is in the middle of a discussion with my mom, apparently talking about her family.

"Hey, Mark," Kara says as we enter the room.

My mom looks up.

"Mom, this is my friend, Mark. Remember, he came to the States tournament with Reese."

"Oh, yes. Hello."

"Hi, how are you?" Mark says. I can tell he's nervous.

"Is Pepper being a good girl?" she says as Mark continues to hold her. "Pepper, be nice."

"What the heck?" Kara says. "Pepper never comes to me."

"She's a brat," I say.

"Yeah, she can be a little grouchy," my mom says. "Especially around little kids. You have to watch she doesn't bite."

"She looks like the Snuggle bear," Reese says. My mom laughs. "Right? The bear from those detergent commercials."

"Or she looks like a rat," I say.

"Yeah, I'd go with that too," Kara says.

I laugh. "I love how much you hate her, Kara."

"She hated me first. Speaking of rats, didn't Pepper eat rat poison once or something and almost die?"

"Not once," I say. "Twice."

"What?" Reese says.

"That was years ago," my mom says after laughing. "We had it in the basement and she got into it. Luckily we took her to the vet in time."

"Then it happened again?" Mark asks.

"Yes, Mark. You might be wondering how that could have happened again because surely my mom removed the rat poison from the basement…no."

"I didn't think she'd eat it *again*! Who's dumb enough to do that?"

"The answer to that question is a dog," I say. "Then one time my sister accidentally stepped on her leg and it broke."

"I remember that," Reese says.

"I'm starting to see why Pepper is a brat," Mark says. "She's had a tough life."

"No excuse," Kara says. "Wait a minute. Weren't you guys supposed to get your housing assignments this week?"

"Yep, we got them," Reese says. "I'm in a scholars dorm, and Brendan's in an honors dorm. My mom tells me the scholars program is just as good as honors."

"Totally," I say sarcastically.

"Are your dorms close to each other?" Mark asks.

"Shockingly, yes," I say. "They're both on north campus."

"You both have one roommate?" Kara asks.

"Two," I say.

Over the next hour or so, more of my friends arrive. In total, about twenty-five people show up, although some just stopped by briefly before heading to another party.

"Okay," Mark says to me as we're all sitting outside on my deck, "what I'm about to say is not trying to belittle your feelings, so don't get upset."

"You know I'm not easily upset."

"From what I saw, your mom actually seems pretty cool."

"It's interesting. I somewhat agree with you. Personality-wise, I think she is pretty uncensored, and it's neat that you don't have to watch what you say around her or be on your best behavior, because she's not stuffy like that. I would hate it if my friends felt like they had to be all prim and proper around her. But regardless of that, she and I still have our major issues. Obviously you've heard plenty of stories from me. It's weird because she and I get along better when we're in a group, like tonight. When it's just us two, it's like we're closed off."

"That's interesting. And I could see how her being uncensored could lead to comments that are hurtful when it's just you two."

"Right. She speaks without thinking. I've realized that it's not just with me. She says things to my sisters too that really get under their skin. Glad I'm not in it alone.

"And you noticed that she said literally one word to you tonight, right?" I continue. "You were one of the first people to get here, and she didn't ask how we knew each other or anything. She didn't ask me about you when came to see me play at States either. It's because she doesn't want to know. But I should try to complain less because it could be a lot worse. And I think our relationship will get better as I get older."

I clear some of the plates and plasticware that have accumulated outside. Mark joins me in my cleaning activities while the rest of my friends continue chatting and laughing.

"Oh my gosh. We have alone time," I whisper to him after we walk into my kitchen together.

"Where's your mom?"

"Upstairs in her room. She's there for the night."

"Are you having fun?" he asks.

"I'm having a blast. I'm in heaven right now."

"I know you told me to try to not think about this, but tonight has reminded me how much I'm going to miss you next year."

"And by 'next year,' you mean 'three weeks'?"

"Agh! Stop!"

"But you know what?" I say. "Senior year is going to be awesome for you, and hopefully freshman year will be the same for me. And we will have a lot of stories to share with each other—new adventures, new experiences…"

He nods. "That's true. And we'll have privacy when I visit you…well, except for your two roommates."

I laugh. "Oh, right. Them."

"When we got back together in May, did you think we'd make it this far?" he asks. I pause to think. "You didn't."

"Let me think. I was cautiously optimistic, but it took time for me to be convinced that things could really work. Not because I doubted us, but because of the secrets and the sneaking around...oh, and your paranoia, of course."

"Which has decreased significantly."

As we head back outside, I think about what Mark said about missing me next year. As I look at my closest friends talking and laughing, I think about how, in a few weeks, I will be leaving so many of them. Leaving the people with whom I have shared my favorite moments in life.

No matter how much I want things to stay the same, it's impossible for that to happen. Friendships will evolve and people will change. I can only hope that everyone here tonight, especially Mark, will be part of the upcoming chapter of my life.

Mark catches my eye, taking me out of my trance. His face asks if I'm okay. I give him a smile and nod. I'm definitely okay. Seeing him reminds me of that. I may not know what the future holds, but I do know that in this moment, I couldn't be happier.

About the Author

The youngest of six kids (and the only boy!), Brian McNamara was born and raised in the suburbs of Cleveland, Ohio. His favorite hobbies growing up were tennis and musical theater. He obtained a degree in finance in 2009 and moved to New York City shortly after to work for a management consulting firm. Using his own high school experience as inspiration for his debut novel, he is thrilled to publish *Bottled Up Secret* with BSB.

Soliloquy Titles From Bold Strokes Books

Maxine Wore Black by Nora Olsen. Jayla will do anything for Maxine, the girl of her dreams, but after becoming ensnared in Maxine's dark secrets, she'll have to choose between love and her own life. (978-1-62639-208-3)

Bottled Up Secret by Brian McNamara. When Brendan Madden befriends his gorgeous, athletic classmate, Mark, it doesn't take long for Brendan to fall head over heels for him—but will Mark reciprocate the feelings? (978-1-62639-209-0)

Searching for Grace by Juliann Rich. First it's a rumor. Then it's a fact. And then it's on. (978-1-62639-196-3)

Dark Tide by Greg Herren. A summer working as a lifeguard at a hotel on the Gulf Coast seems like a dream job…until Ricky Hackworth realizes the town is shielding some very dark—and deadly—secrets. (978-1-62639-197-0)

Everything Changes by Samantha Hale. Raven Walker's world is turned upside down the moment Morgan O'Shea walks into her life. (978-1-62639-303-5)

Fifty Yards and Holding by David Matthew-Barnes. The discovery of a secret relationship between Riley Brewer, the star of the high school baseball team, and Victor Alvarez, the leader of a violent street gang, escalates into a preventable tragedy. (978-1-62639-081-2)

Tristant and Elijah by Jennifer Lavoie. After Elijah finds a scandalous letter belonging to Tristant's great-uncle, the boys set out to discover the secret Uncle Glenn kept hidden his entire life and end up discovering who they are in the process. (978-1-62639-075-1)

Caught in the Crossfire by Juliann Rich. Two boys at Bible camp; one forbidden love. (978-1-62639-070-6)

Frenemy of the People by Nora Olsen. Clarissa and Lexie have despised each other for as long as they can remember, but when they both find themselves helping an unlikely contender for homecoming queen, they are catapulted into an unexpected romance. (978-1-62639-063-8)

The Balance by Neal Wooten. Love and survival come together in the distant future as Piri and Niko face off against the worst factions of mankind's evolution. (978-1-62639-055-3)

The Unwanted by Jeffrey Ricker. Jamie Thomas is plunged into danger when he discovers his mother is an Amazon who needs his help to save the tribe from a vengeful god. (978-1-62639-048-5)

Because of Her by KE Payne. When Tabby Morton is forced to move to London, she's convinced her life will never be the same again. But the beautiful and intriguing Eden Palmer is about to show her that this time, change is most definitely for the better. (978-1-62639-049-2)

The Seventh Pleiade by Andrew J. Peters. When Atlantis is besieged by violent storms, tremors, and a barbarian army, it will be up to a young gay prince to find a way for the kingdom's survival. (978-1-60282-960-2)

Asher's Fault by Elizabeth Wheeler. Fourteen-year-old Asher Price sees the world in black and white, much like the photos he takes, but when his little brother drowns at the same moment Asher experiences his first same-sex kiss, he can no longer hide behind the lens of his camera and eventually discovers he isn't the only one with a secret. (978-1-60282-982-4)

Meeting Chance by Jennifer Lavoie. When man's best friend turns on Aaron Cassidy, the teen keeps his distance until fate puts Chance in his hands. (978-1-60282-952-7)

Lake Thirteen by Greg Herren. A visit to an old cemetery seems like fun to a group of five teenagers, who soon learn that sometimes it's best to leave old ghosts alone. (978-1-60282-894-0)